RELL'S KISS

LAUELE FRACTURED FOLKTALES #2

LEHUA PARKER

MAKENA PRESS

RELL'S KISS
by
Lehua Parker

Rell's Kiss is a work of fiction. Names, characters, places and incidents either are the product of the author's imagination or are used fictitiously. Any resemblance to actual persons living or dead, events, or locales is entirely coincidental.

For information on subsidiary rights, please contact the author at:

AuntyLehua@LehuaParker.com

An earlier version of this story titled *Rell Goes Hawaiian* was published by Tork Media in *Fractured Slipper*, a collection of stories based on *Cinderella*.

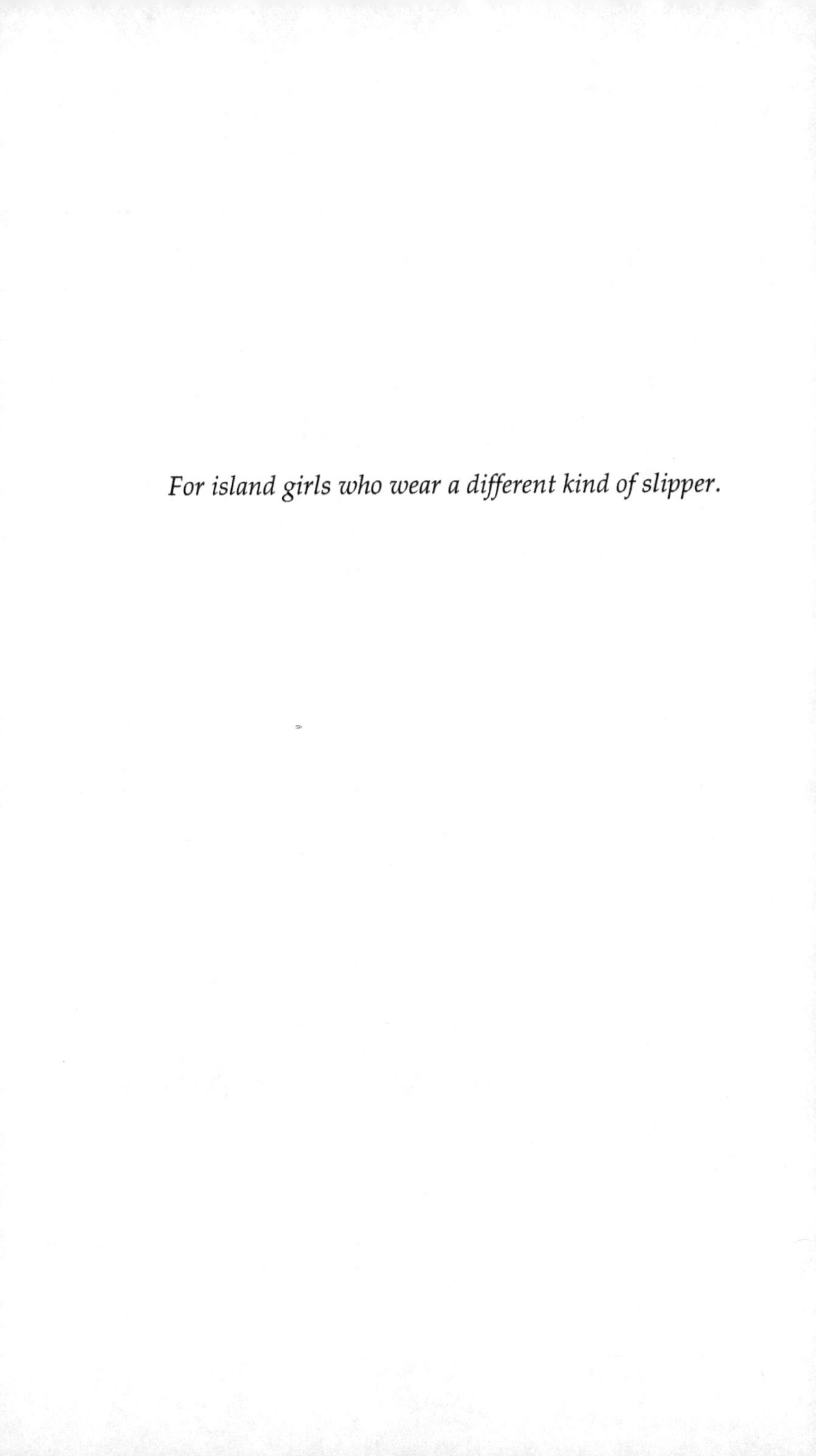

For island girls who wear a different kind of slipper.

The rental agent in the beige cargo shorts and electric green polo shirt shakes his head. "No matter how hard you cram, it's not going to fit."

I'm standing in the parking lot of Aloha Island Rentals at the Honolulu International Airport and trying not to cry. Next to me are twin stacks of boxes piled higher than my shoulders, each stamped with Watanabe Global—Rush Delivery—Extremely Fragile.

Looking at the orange Mini Cooper convertible in front of me, I'd be hard pressed to fit even my single carry-on in the trunk.

I have less than two hours to get everything across the island before my wicked stepmonster erupts and rains hot lava all over me.

Who am I kidding? Even if I pull off this miracle, she'll still blow her top.

Rental Dude waves his sales tablet over the mess like a magic wand and says, "You're going to need something much larger. Why'd your company reserve this car?"

I sigh. "Because I asked for it."

"A Mini?"

"A convertible. I had this image of driving through paradise with the top down."

"You didn't know about the boxes?" he asks.

"Nope. This is Regina's way of getting back at me."

"Regina—"

"Regina Watanabe."

"Of Watanabe Global?"

"Yep."

"You're her assistant?"

"Stepdaughter."

He checks his tablet. "The reservation is for R. Watanabe."

"That's me. The R is for Rell, not Regina."

"Got it. You're here for the auction?"

I nod.

"The whole island's talking about it. It's a big deal," he says.

Somehow, this is all going to be my fault.

Don't cry, don't cry, don't cry, I tell myself.

Out loud I say, "The Mini isn't going to work. Talk to me about renting a truck or van."

He tippy-taps on his tablet for a moment and frowns.

"We don't have anything available on the lot. I have a van due back later tonight, but that's not soon enough for the auction." A few more taps. "Looks like none of the other agencies have trucks or vans available, either."

I feel tears start to well again, but there's no way I'm going to let something Regina did make me cry. When Daddy died six years ago, I swore whatever happened, I'd never give her that satisfaction again.

She thinks banishing me to a tiny all-girls prep school in North Dakota is torture, but I know the Christmases and summers I spent on campus with the headmaster's family were warmer than any celebration at home.

Wherever that is.

I almost feel sorry for my ten-year-old stepsisters, Zel and Ana.

Almost.

Today's date is just a coincidence. I should've known when Regina sent me the ticket to Hawaii that this trip wasn't about me. The car and boxes prove that.

Stepmonsters never change their stripes.

I bite my lip hard. There's got to be a way.

"What about a delivery service? Can I hire someone to take the boxes to La...La...?"

"It's pronounced *Lau-el-lay*. Lauele."

"Lauele," I say. "Thanks."

He pushes back the brim of his cap with his stylus. "The auction's not really in Lauele, though. It's at a pavilion above Keikikai Beach. That's where they're setting up the tents for the auction and luau. Is that where the boxes need to go?"

I nod.

He looks at the ground for a moment, then makes a decision.

"Hey, I know we just met, and I don't want you to think I'm some kind of creeper—"

Said every creeper ever.

I take half a step back.

He sees the look on my face and laughs. "Which is exactly what a creeper would say?"

I shrug.

Pretty much.

"Just hear me out. You don't have many options, and there are a ton of boxes."

"What do you have in mind?"

He points toward the monkeypod tree in the employee lot. "Take my truck."

What? He can't be serious. Who does that?

"Take your truck?" I say. "I can't do that."

"Why not? I'm offering."

I raise an eyebrow, considering. He's about my age, maybe a couple of years older. He's taller than me, the kind of taller where you can wear fancy heels on a date, but don't have to stand on your toes to kiss.

Kiss? Right. Like I'd know anything about that.

What I read in books and magazines doesn't count.

My eyes travel across his broad shoulders, down to his slim waist, and quickly back to his face.

Get a grip, Rell. Look at his eyes, not his body. You're the one who's acting creepy about this.

His green eyes widen when I meet them.

Oh, great. He knows I've been checking him out.

His uniform is hardly stylish, but he makes it work. Wisps of sun-streaked hair peek out from the edges of his cap.

My stomach flips. *He's cute. How did I miss this?*

Oh, yeah. The boxes.

Focus, Rell!

I swallow and point. "That truck?"

"Yeah. The Datsun with the surf racks. Don't laugh. It's paid for."

I feel the blush rise. "No! I mean, it's great—"

He laughs again. "Relax. I'm just teasing. It may not look like much, but it runs well. You can drive a stick, right?"

My heart sinks.

"No."

"Good, because it's an automatic. You have no excuse."

His eyes are full of mischief. This is too easy. Nothing involving my stepmonster is ever easy. I'm missing something.

"Why are you getting involved? This isn't your problem."

He flicks his stylus against his tablet. "I'm from Lauele, born and raised. Watanabe Global is a major sponsor of the new International Abilities Surf Camp."

"I think they're announcing some kind of partnership with Get Wet Prosthetics tonight," I say.

"Get Wet started the International Abilities Surf Tournament. Jay Westin—you know Jay?"

"No."

"He's a close friend. I've surfed with him since boogie board days. The surf camp is Jay's idea. He wants to make it easy for kids with disabilities to learn to surf."

"That's amazing," I say. "I don't know much about the camp at all."

"When I left Lauele this morning, the crew from Get

Wet was already busy setting up. They're probably waiting on this stuff."

"Regina's text said I had to get the boxes delivered before noon."

He reaches out and pats a box. "Take my truck and get your boxes delivered. If makes you feel better, I'm not helping you; I'm helping my friend, Jay."

There's something wrong with this. Finally, I see it.

"But if I take your truck, how will you get home?"

"Me? Bus. With stops, it's only a four hour trip."

My mouth drops. I can't let him do that.

Laughter bubbles out of him like water from a fountain.

"I'm not taking the bus, Rell. I'll drive the Mini Cooper home and meet you later. We'll trade. I'm off in a couple of hours."

He pauses, waiting for me to agree.

I stand in the sunshine looking at the stacks of boxes. I so want to leave them. I'm tired of Regina's passive-aggressive crap.

"Of course, if you have another option…" he says.

All those boxes.

He's right. Leaving the boxes would only hurt the auction, not Regina. The truck's old and worn, but it should do the trick. As weird as this is, I don't think it's a scam.

Okay. I'm doing it.

I fumble in my purse. "I don't have a lot of cash with me—"

He pushes my hand away from my wallet.

"Nonsense," he says. "I'm not taking your money." He crosses his arms and frowns. "Stop trying to make this complicated, Rell. It's very simple. You need to get those boxes to Lauele. I have a truck. It's cool."

I throw up my hands. "This is insane."

He laughs. "Insane is trying to shoehorn those boxes into a Mini Cooper. It's really no big deal. I'm happy to help. C'mon. Let's finish up the paperwork, load the truck, and get you on the road."

2

Back at the rental office, he runs around the counter and brings up the forms on a monitor.

"Where are you staying? Waikiki? I know it's not in Lauele. There aren't any hotels out there."

"We're staying somewhere close. It's the private residence of someone my stepmother knows." I grab my phone and pull up the address. "It's called Hale O Ka Poliahu."

"No way. You know Poliahu?"

I blink, wondering at his tone. "Uh, no. I think she's someone my stepmother met while skiing in Switzerland. When news got out about Watanabe Global sponsoring the auction for the surf camp, Poliahu offered us her home. She said staying there would be easier than driving back and forth across the island."

"She's right. Lauele is not a tourist-y kind of place. Not a lot of services out there. But, wow. You hit the jackpot. Poliahu's estate is legendary."

"You know it?"

He shakes his head. "By reputation only." He hits enter a few times as the screen flashes. "The house sits upcountry in the mountains above Keikikai Beach. It's usually empty. I can't remember the last time Poliahu was home."

The printer under the counter whirls, spitting out the rental contract. "Okay. One Mini Cooper Convertible. Two day rental. Aw, seems like a shame to fly all this way and only stay two days."

"Believe me, two days with my family is long enough."

He pauses, then lightly touches my hand. "I'm sorry," he says.

I shrug. "It is what it is. It's fine."

With a highlighter, he marks up the contract. "Since it's a corporate rental, here's where the collision insurance and extra driver fees are waved. Be sure to bring it back full, or we'll have to charge you extra for the fuel. Initial here, here, and here. Sign there. I just need your driver's license, and we're done."

I really don't want to hand him my license, but I have no choice. Reading the signs posted all over the office, I realize why the reservation's under R. Watanabe and booked under Regina's account. This is the moment when he tells me I can't rent a car at all. One last calculated humiliation by Regina, I'm sure.

Maybe he'll tell me how to catch the bus.

I keep my finger over my birthdate as I slide my license across the counter, but when he picks it up, he sees it anyway.

"Hey! Today's your birthday! Hau'ole la hanau."

I blush.

Again.

"Thanks," I mumble. "Is this a problem?"

He double-checks it. "For a regular rental, you're underage. We make exceptions for corporate rentals."

Hallelujah!

I let the air I was holding out in a rush.

He hands my license back with a sympathetic smile. "It's a silly rule. Most of the guys who work here are under 25, and we drive the cars all the time."

He throws me the keys from his pocket and grabs the keys to the Mini off the rack. We walk back through the rental lot to his truck parked in shade of a big monkeypod tree. He opens the door for me, and I climb in.

"Don't worry. It's rusty and a little dinged up, but my truck's safe. Just make sure you brake extra hard and pump 'em a bit before you stop."

"What!"

"Kidding, kidding! The brakes are fine. Man, you make teasing too easy." He slams the door and the whole cab rattles. I start the engine. Warm air blasts from the vents. I look for the button to roll down the widows.

He taps on the glass and points.

It's a hand crank.

I roll the window down.

Literally.

It takes forever.

The whole time he's grinning at me.

"Good," he says when the window's open. "I wasn't sure if you knew what that was. There's no air-conditioning, so you'll want to keep the windows rolled down. Just think of it as driving a convertible with a roof." He pats the hood. "Meet me at the boxes."

I adjust the rearview and figure out how to put it in gear. When I'm at the far side of the parking lot, I surreptitiously test the brakes.

No problem. The truck's bigger than what I'm used to, but it handles well.

I pull up next to the boxes and leave the truck idling. It doesn't take long to load them. Rather than stick my bag next to me, I slip it in the back behind the cab and in front of the boxes.

For a moment, I stand there a little dazed and overwhelmed. I'm not quite sure how all this came together.

"Know where you're going?" he asks.

I hold up my phone. "I've got the address. Google Maps should get me there."

He holds up a finger. "I almost forgot. Wait just one sec."

He dashes back inside and comes back with a business card and a lei made of shiny black seeds. "Here's my phone number. Call if you have any problems. I can leave work early if you need me."

"My number is—"

He wiggles his phone. "Got it off the paperwork. I'll text when I get back to Lauele this afternoon."

I look at the neatly stacked boxes and shake my head.

"Is this what they mean by the aloha spirit?"

He gives me a look like he's not sure where I'm going with this. "Isn't this just doing the right thing? That's universal, no?"

No. But thank goodness I'm in Hawaii.

"I don't even know your name," I say.

He holds out his hand. "Jerry Santos."

I take it. It's warm and strong and slightly rough.

"Rell Watanabe."

He grips my hand tighter and pulls me a little closer. He places the lei around my neck. "

Aloha, Rell," he says, pecking me on the cheek. "Welcome to Hawaii."

3

"**Y**ou're late."

When I step out of the truck, I ignore my stepmonster for a moment and take in the view. From the driveway, I can see all the way down the mountainside to the beach and out to sea. Waves that look like squiggly lines roll to the sand. If I squint, I can see surfers riding to the shore. The air is chilly, far chillier than I ever imagined Hawaii would be. I puff out a breath, expecting to see it turn to frost like it does back home in winter, but it doesn't.

"What happened to the convertible you insisted on? Don't tell me you'd rather drive this—" I don't have to look. I know how her mouth twists over these words —"whatever it is."

I turn to her and force a smile. "Hi Regina. It's nice to see you again."

She snorts, but keeps her eyes from rolling. "Those boxes don't belong here. I told you to take them to the venue. That means the place where the auction is being held, not the house where we're staying. I'll try not to use such big words in the future."

"I know what venue means, I just—"

She sighs. "It's hard for you to think of others, I know, but please remember we're guests here. No doubt that jalopy is leaking oil on Poliahu's beautiful driveway."

"If it's leaking oil, I'll scrub it."

"With what? Your toothbrush? Honestly, Rell, if you'd use your brain for once—just move the truck. Don't be so dramatic."

The front door crashes open, and Zel and Ana come tumbling out, chasing a gray tabby.

"Get him!" Zel shrieks.

"I got the rope. You tie the noose," Ana shouts.

Noose? No way. I didn't hear that right.

Zel lunges for the cat, but misses. "I told you I'm not doing the noose again, Ana. You have to learn how to tie it yourself."

"But you know what happened last time, Zel. You do it."

"No."

The cat starts left, then jukes right, fleeing between Ana's legs.

"You're letting him get away!" Zel says.

"Anastasia! Drizella!" Regina shouts. "I told you to leave that filthy animal alone. You'll get fleas."

The cat escapes over a rock wall and disappears under a bush.

"Aw, Mom," they chorus. "You never let us have any fun."

Good grief. My stepsisters are monsters.

"Enough. I am not getting held up in customs again because you two have fleas."

Zel pouts and scratches her arm. "It wasn't fleas, it was—"

Regina holds up her hand. "Don't argue. You want fun? Fine. Go change. Rell's taking you to the beach."

What?

"Me?"

"Yes, you. You're already dressed for it in those ragged shorts and t-shirt. I hope you didn't embarrass yourself by wearing that on the plane."

Zel snickers. "I bet she wore that on the plane."

Ana says, "Not in first class!"

Brats!

I look at my cut-offs and t-shirt. "What's wrong with my clothes?"

"Rell, the real question is what's right?" Regina snips. "They're hardly couture. They're fine for house cleaning, I suppose, although I don't really know."

"Or going to the beach," Ana says.

"You promised fun, Mom," Zel says.

I look at the twins. Growing up under Regina, they really didn't stand a chance.

It's not their fault.

I can play nice.

"You really want me to take them to the beach?"

Regina says, "Yes. But first move the truck and sign the papers."

"What papers?"

"Why must you question everything I say? Get a move on. You haven't got all day."

She spins on her heel and heads to the house.

"Girls, let's go. Mommy has lots to do. Unlike Rell, Mommy's busy, busy, busy. A lollygagger, that's what Rell is. But she's here now to take care of you."

"Is lollygagger French for nanny?" asks Zel.

"No, dummy," says Ana. "She's not our nanny. She's old Papa Watanabe's daughter."

"But he's dead."

"Yeah," says Ana, picking at a scab on her arm. "He's worm food now."

"So if she's not our new nanny, why is she here?" Zel asks.

Ana shrugs. "I dunno. Maybe she wants something."

"My new iPhone? She can't have that."

Regina grabs each of the twins by the arm and hisses. "Rell is nothing for you to worry about. She wants nothing; she gets nothing. She's just here for a couple of days, one night only, then she's going back to school, and you'll never see her again. Now go change!"

She marches them to the door and shoves them into the house. Pausing on the threshold, she points to the truck and then to the street before slamming the door hard enough to rattle the glass.

I close my eyes. "Two days is an eternity."

"Meow?"

I bend down and look under the bushes. "Kitty-kitty," I say. Gray fuzz peeps out at me. "It's okay, sweetie. They've gone. I won't let them hurt you."

"Prraow?"

I hold out my hand, and the cat slinks over and rubs against me. I pick her up, and she melts, her purr vibrating so deeply in her chest that it tingles against my shoulder.

"At least somebody's happy to see me."

The cat snuggles deeper, warming me until I'm no longer shivering. I need to get my jacket out of my bag.

A red cardinal swoops by, flitting from branch to branch in the tree above me.

"Look at you! You're gorgeous," I say.

He preens and trills.

I laugh. "Now you're just showing off." He bobs his head and shakes his tail.

A monarch butterfly lands on the roof of the truck, the black and orange patterns of his wings blurring in the sunlight like—

"Oil!"

I put the cat down and hurry to park on the street.

Jerry's truck runs fine, but I'm not taking a chance.

I only have one toothbrush.

4

I set the parking brake, grab my jacket from my bag in the back, and walk slowly up the driveway. I hesitate, then enter the house through the servant's side door.

"Hello?" I call.

My stepmonster answers from the dining room. "We're in here," she sighs, "Waiting on you, as usual, Rell. But take your time. It's not like we've other, more important things to do."

In the dining room, at one end of a long dining table sits three men, two in crisp aloha shirts and khakis and one in a three-piece wool suit and tie. There are stacks of papers piled high on the table and several pens lined up next to an empty chair.

Regina nervously hovers, fidgeting with her pearls. I narrow my eyes. She's never nervous.

On the table are official-looking stamps, seals, and ink pads. Behind the men on the buffet table are more file boxes stuffed with millions of folders.

Except for the warm wood furnishings, everything is in shades of white. White gardenias float in crystal bowls, their scent cool and clean. Snowy linens cover the table.

Even wearing my jacket, I shiver. Somehow the beautiful room comes off as cold as a mountain peak. The vibe is Hawaiian-Eskimo, something weirdly anti-tropical. Looking out the window, I half-expect to see a snow-dusted coconut tree.

At the far side of the room in front of a fireplace are two chairs and a table arranged for a cozy tête-à-tête. The fireplace is big enough to roast an ox.

We need a fire to warm things up. Heaven knows we have enough paper here to burn down the house.

Twice.

Regina places her palm on the back of a chair and raps her ring against it, the sound like a judge's gavel.

"Sit here, Rell. Let's get started."

I pull out the chair. It's heavier than it looks and slides awkwardly along the thick carpet. I sit, and the man in the three-piece suit turns to me. "Rell, we've met before—"

"When I was twelve. I remember."

He continues as if I'm invisible. "My name is Michael Lucius. I'm an attorney with Lucius, Griffin, and Melton. These are my associates, Avery Me'e and Mark Andrews. Do you know why you're here?"

"No."

"Yes, you do," Regina says. "It's your birthday."

"You remembered! Wait. Are you throwing me a surprise party? Is that why you brought me to Hawaii?"

"No."

"You're teasing. My surprise party is the luau tonight! I knew the charity auction couldn't be real."

Regina's lips press into a thin white line.

Awesome. Now if I can just get her eye to twitch…

I say, "Oh, no. Did I ruin the surprise?"

The corner of her eye jumps. *Yes!*

"Rell, not everything is about you. The auction tonight has nothing to do with your birthday."

Of course not. I know better than to expect a party. But the surf camp doesn't make sense. Charity's not Regina's thing.

I wink. "Got it. No birthday luau."

Regina takes a deep breath. "You're here to sign papers, that's all."

"And deliver boxes. Don't forget that part."

She squints and pinches the bridge of her nose. With any luck, I've given her a migraine.

"That's enough," she says. "No one likes a drama queen. You sign papers every year on your birthday."

Yeah, in the school secretary's office. It's no big deal. This feels like a big deal.

"Not in Hawaii," I say.

"You're complaining about a trip to Hawaii? Unbelievable. Nothing I do makes you happy. You even disliked the convertible."

"Yeah, thanks for arranging that. So thoughtful."

Regina throws her hands in the air. "See? Do you see what I deal with? Clearly, this is why we're here today, gentlemen."

Mr. Lucius delicately coughs. "If I may? Rell, it's exactly as your stepmother said. You're here to sign a paper. The process today is much like what's happened in the preceding years, but with a little more formality. Mr. Andrews is a notary. As Regina is your guardian, Mr. Me'e and I will serve as witnesses to your signature. Everything is in order."

Mr. Andrews nods and holds up his notary seal. "I need to see your driver's license for my records. We all know who you are, but contracts are contracts. We must obey the law."

For the second time today, I hand a stranger my ID and watch as he copies information from it. Stamp, stamp, sign, double-sign, date, and he's done.

"As a Notary Public, I certify that the young lady in front of me is Rell H. Watanabe," he says.

"Thank you, Mr. Andrews," says Regina. "Let's get on with it."

As I slide my driver's license back into my wallet, Jerry's business card falls out.

"What's that?" Regina asks.

"Nothing," I say, tucking it back in as my heart beats wildly. "Just a card from the rental place."

To hide my reaction, I reach for the stack of papers nearest me. "Do I have to sign all of these?"

Mr. Lucius chuckles. "No, my dear. That would take hours. We've simplified it for you. You just have to sign one document." He takes the papers from me and flips to the back where a post-it flag sticks out. "We only need your signature here. I've already dated it."

I pick up a pen and scan the page.

"Mr. Me'e and Mr. Lucius already signed the witness lines," I say.

"Of course. Unlike you, they are sensitive about wasting other people's time," Regina says. "Sign and let these good people get on with their day, Rell."

Her tone is annoyed, but her face is eerily blank.

Something's off.

I flip a couple of pages.

"What am I signing?"

Regina rolls her eyes, but her facial expression doesn't change. "I told you. Papers that allow me to continue to pay for your schooling. You want that, right?"

I turn and look up at her. "Smile," I say.

"What?" she sputters.

No change.

"Smile."

"You ungrateful little—"

No change.

"Are you upset with me?" I ask. "I really can't tell if you're mad or happy or sad—"

The penny drops.

Her face has been Botox'd to the max. I peer closer. That's a new nose. The flab under her chin has definitely been tightened, too.

She's not happy or sad. She's annoyed as always, but plastic surgery has taken care of both the wrinkles and the emotion. Even her skin looks waxy.

Whatever.

I turn back to the document.

"Mr. Me'e, does signing this paper allow me to graduate high school in the spring and start college in the fall?"

Mr. Lucius shoots him a look and says, "This is not a negotiation."

Negotiation? All I've asked is a simple yes/no question.

Mr. Me'e says, "It allows—"

Regina snaps, "Do you want me to pay your tuition

or not? That's what it comes down to, Rell. Sign it, and things go on exactly as they have before."

"It that correct, Mr. Me'e?"

Mr. Me'e says, "Signing will—"

"Yes," says Mr. Lucius. "If you sign the document, Regina can continue to pay for your schooling."

"There are other options," Mr. Me'e says.

"Yes, she can be homeless. She can get a GED. She can get a job as fry cook. Or she can complete her education in comfort. It doesn't matter to me. I try to do a good thing, and it's turning into a mess. Typical. Sign or not, but stop wasting everyone's valuable time, Rell," Regina says.

"But with all these papers, it seems like—"

Regina shakes her head as she reaches over and snatches the pen out of my hand. "I'm sorry, gentlemen. This has been a colossal waste of time. Apparently, Rell feels the need to read each and every scrap of paper before signing."

Wait a minute.

"I just want to know—"

"We told you, but, as always, you're not listening. You're complaining that I brought you to Hawaii instead of letting you stay at school and sign the papers there." She turns to Mr. Lucius. "You're right. I should've anticipated this. She was always such a diffi-cult, suspicious child."

"I am not."

"See?" Regina says.

Mr. Me'e says, "Do you want me to explain—"

"Lucius," Regina interrupts, "contact her school this

afternoon and tell them next month's tuition and dorm fees can't be paid."

"Yes, Regina."

Mr. Me'e starts to speak, but Regina stops him again.

"She's stubborn and foolish, Mr. Me'e." Regina waves her hand at all the mountains of paper. "There's no way Rell can read through everything before the payments are due. As you know, without her signature, my hands are tied when it comes to disbursing funds on her behalf."

Mr. Me'e says, "That's true, however—"

Regina cuts him off again. "I appreciate your concern for her welfare, even if she doesn't. Your heart is in the right place, Mr. Me'e, but if Rell insists on being uneducated and out on the street, it's her choice."

Mr. Lucius stands. "I think we're done here today, gentlemen."

Regina shakes Mr. Lucius's hand. "Thank you again. I'll be in touch. Rell, see them out. It's the least you can do."

Regina pivots and exits the room.

I look at the document.

Sign or be homeless and uneducated.

I'm not going to cry. She can't make me cry.

Life doesn't have to be like this.

Next year, I'm going to college. I'll get out from under Regina's thumb. I'll scrub dishes and wait tables if I have to.

But first I have to graduate from high school.

The pages blur, but I manage to pick up a pen, find the signature line, and scrawl my name across it.

The men stand up. Mr. Me'e sighs as he picks up the papers. Regina rushes back into the room.

"She signed?"

Mr. Me'e holds it up.

"I want a copy of that for my records. Several copies, in fact," Regina says. "Put the original in the vault."

"Avery?" Mr. Lucius says.

Mr. Me'e places the signed paper in his briefcase and locks it. "Consider it done. I'll have the copies delivered tomorrow."

"Mommy," says a voice, "I thought Rell was taking us to the beach."

Zel and Ana stand in the doorway, wearing the most hideous swimsuits I've ever seen, all ruffles and bows.

With their frizzy hair, they look like overdressed poodles at a clown convention.

Ridiculous.

The stress gets to me, and I can't help it.

I laugh.

"Mom!" yips Ana. "What's wrong with Rell?"

Yips. Like a poodle.

I throw my head back and howl.

"Nothing, dear. She's just deliriously happy to see you." Her tone is angry, but Regina's face doesn't change.

Oh, man. She has resting witch face. And she did it on purpose.

I almost fall out of the chair.

Mr. Lucius reaches for the pitcher on the sideboard. "Maybe a glass of water would help?"

Laughter burns the anger and sadness away. I feel much better.

"No," I say. "It's okay. I'm fine."

Snort, giggle.

I swallow hard.

Get a grip, Rell. Keep it up and the next thing you know you'll be locked away in an insane asylum.

I rub my eyes and take a breath. "Those boxes need to get to the *venue*. The rental car guy told me that's at a pavilion above Keikikai Beach. Is that a good place for the girls to swim?"

"Yes. It's one of the best family beaches on the island," Mr. Me'e says.

I open my mouth and a hiccup escapes. "Excuse me. That red-eye flight was long. But flights are cheaper after midnight, right?"

The barb goes right over Regina's head. I've been dismissed and forgotten like yesterday's dishes.

It's not worth a sigh.

"Zel and Ana, let's give Regina some peace and quiet so she can get her work done before the party. It's beach time. Not even paperwork can ruin a day at the beach."

The girls don't say anything until after they climb in truck, and we're heading down the mountain to the beach.

"Ana says you're not our new nanny."

"No, Zel, I'm your big sister," I say.

"Stepsister," Ana says.

I shoot her a look. "Right. Stepsister. I know it's been a long time since we've seen each other. I think you guys were just four—"

"If you're not our new nanny, why are you taking us to the beach?" Zel asks.

"Don't you want to go to the beach? It's fun."

Ana shrugs her shoulders. "Whatever."

"Whatever," says Zel.

"Your mom told me to take you to the beach."

"Whatever," Ana says again. "But remember, just because you're driving, you're not the boss of us."

"Yeah. The last nanny thought she was the boss of us," Zel says.

"Nanny Bossy didn't last long," Ana says, staring out the window. "We Nair'd her."

"Nair'd her?" I ask.

"In her shampoo."

"You didn't!" I gasp.

Zel nods. "We did. Now she's Nanny Baldo."

Ana scrunches up her face. "More like Nanny Patches."

I give them another look. "So how bossy was she?"

Ana turns to me. "She wanted us to pick our clothes up off the floor."

"And read books."

"And took away our candy."

"We NEED our candy."

"So don't try to take it," Ana says.

"Okay," I say and try not to scratch my suddenly itchy head.

When we hit the highway that circumnavigates the island, I turn right and follow the signs to Lauele. The ocean peeps through the ironwood trees on the left, but it's not until we come to a two-story building with a big sign saying Hari's on the front that the view really opens up.

Across the street from Hari's is a beach pavilion with a sign that reads Keikikai Beach. Big delivery trucks fill the parking lot. In a grassy field people are setting up a big event tent and an on-site catering kitchen.

"Must be the place," I say, pulling into the parking lot.

Zel points to the big banner across the front of the

tent: International Abilities Surf Camp Charity Auction & Luau.

"You think?"

Ana rolls her eyes. "You're right, Zel. She's too stupid to be our nanny."

"Hey!"

They jump out of the truck and start heading toward the beach.

"Zel! Ana! What about all the boxes?"

Without stopping, they wave at me.

"Not our problem," Zel says over her shoulder.

"That's why you're here," Ana says.

"And your truck smells like old feet!" Zel shouts.

I scramble out of the truck. I almost forget, but at the last minute I grab my purse off the seat and whip it over my head and across my body. The girls are striding across the sand now. "Zel! Ana! Get back—"

"Jerry, you can't park here."

I whirl around.

Nobody's there.

"What?" I say.

I hear a tongue click and a sigh. "Down here."

I peer over the hood of the truck. "Oh. Sorry, I didn't see you."

Near the license plate, a tiny man with a clipboard adjusts his hat and frowns. "Why are you driving Jerry Santos's truck? Where's Jerry?"

"I—"

"Never mind. You have to move it. We need the entire parking lot for the event tonight."

"But—"

"Eh, Luna. Check out the back. The wahine brought

the boxes we've been waiting for." Two thick brown hands reach over the side of the truck and lift out a box.

The guy with the clipboard grins. "Why didn't you say so? Hui! Eh, gangies! Come kokua!"

In an instant, one by one the boxes begin to rise out of the truck and float toward the tent.

What the what?

I walk around the front of the truck and into a scene from *Willy Wonka.* A fireman's brigade of men no taller than three feet are unloading the boxes and handing them down the line and into the tent.

The one lifting the boxes out of the back taps the side of the truck. "Eh! Das the last one," he says. "All pau!"

I peek into the back to check, but when I turn around to thank them, they've disappeared.

The first guy rips something from his clipboard and holds it out. "Your receipt."

I glance at it. "Menehune Inc.?"

He grins. "We're Local 808. No job too big or small. We specialize in rock walls. I'm Luna. You a friend of Jerry's?"

"Sort of."

"Ah," he nods. "That kind of friend."

"No!" Heat pinks my cheeks. "He just lent me his truck. That's all."

He cocks his head. "Oooh! You're THAT kind of friend."

I adjust my bag over my shoulder and glare. "I don't know what you're talking about."

"Relax, titah. I'm just joking with you. You work for Watanabe Global, right?"

"Sort of. I'm Rell."

"Ah-ha! I thought I recognized that smell."

"What?"

I fight an impulse to sniff my arm pit. Instead I surreptitiously rub my cheek on my shoulder and breathe deeply.

Flowers and laundry detergent.

This guy's nuts.

He flicks his wrist. "Nothing. You remind me of your mother."

"You knew my mom?"

"Oh, yeah. She was a Mahope. The Mahopes go way back in Lauele. You never know?"

I shake my head. "No."

"Your family owns land around here. It's just mauka of the land where they want to build the surf camp. See?" He points uphill. "That's where the road will go. You seen the designs, yeah?"

I shake my head. "I don't know anything about the project."

"Well, go park Jerry's junkalunka truck in front of Hari's store—he won't mind—and come to the tent. We'll show you everything."

"Thanks, but I can't. The twins took off down to the beach, and I need to keep an eye on them."

Luna whistles. "Makani!"

"Yeah, Luna?" a voice answers.

"Girls. Beach. Now."

"On it!"

I don't see Makani, but I hear feet thunder across the pavement. A heartbeat later, little puffs of sand rise from the beach.

Luna smiles. "No worries. Makani will keep an eye on them."

My stomach clenches. "I don't know Makani."

"No worries. He's like the wind. He'll make sure they don't get into trouble."

"I think I better—"

He taps the side of the truck. "I need you to move this first. After you park the car, go into Hari's store. Tell him Luna wants a sprunch. Put it on my tab."

"Luna, you sly dog. Tell Hari yourself. Don't let this guy fool you, Rell," says a voice behind me.

"Jerry! Don't spoil my fun," Luna says.

My heart skips.

Jerry!

He startled me.

That's it.

That's all.

It has nothing to do with his deep surfer's tan or eyes like green beach glass.

Right.

Jerry holds out his hand. Reflexively I hold mine out, too. He drops keys into my palm.

"I hoped I'd find you here. Your rental car's across the street at Hari's. Are my keys still inside the truck?"

"Yes."

"I'll get my truck out of Luna's hair."

"Thanks so much for loaning it to me. I couldn't have done this without you."

"No problem." He opens the door and climbs in the cab.

I grab the open window before he can shut the door. "Hey. You said you were involved with the surf camp.

Luna was just going to show me the plans. Wanna come see?"

Inside, I groan.

That sounds desperate. Needy. Guys hate that.

"I'd love to. Be right back."

I watch as Jerry backs up and parks across the street next to an orange Mini. I can't stop smiling.

"Oh, yeah," says Luna. "Totally a friend like that."

7

When Jerry jogs back, he's holding a hideous ruffled floral beach wrap. "I think this belongs to you."

I want to die.

"Actually, I think it belongs to one of my stepsisters." I quickly stuff it in my purse. "I really should go check on them."

"Makani's with them," Luna says. "They're fine."

I hesitate.

Jerry comes to my rescue. He jumps up on the rock wall separating the grass from the sand and scans the beach.

"Luna's right. The girls are fine. See for yourself."

He reaches down and pulls me up next to him. He puts a hand on my shoulder and leans close as he points toward the ocean. His aftershave reminds me of cedar and cinnamon.

I breathe deeply.

And a touch of clove.

I shake my head.

This is ridiculous, Rell. You're acting like a lovesick puppy. Knock it off.

Jerry mistakes my headshake for a no.

"Can't see them? Look a little more to the right."

He leans closer until his breath kisses my cheek.

Wintergreen mint.

All I have to do is turn my head, and we'll be kissing for real.

Ah! Focus! Ana and Zel. Where are they?

I follow Jerry's arm as it points out along a lava outcrop. The girls are still close to the main beach, splashing in a shallow tide pool. A few feet away, a medium-sized yellow dog approaches them, wagging its tail.

A dog.

The girls wanted to hang a cat.

This can't be good.

I step away from Jerry, so I can think.

"I see Ana and Zel, but I don't see Makani," I say.

"He's out there. Guaranteed," Luna says.

"Makani's a dog?" I ask.

Luna cocks his head. "A dog? No, Makani's a—"

"She's talking about 'Ilima," Jerry interrupts.

"'Ilima? Who's 'Ilima?" I ask.

"That yellow poi dog next to the girls is named 'Ilima. Between 'Ilima and Makani, the girls are in good hands. There's no need to worry about them," Jerry says.

"Everyone keeps telling me that I don't have to worry because Makani's out there, even though I can't see him. Are you telling me now that 'Ilima's a lifeguard? She'll jump in and rescue the girls if they get swept out to sea?"

"'Ilima's 'Ilima," Luna says, scratching his head. "Makani's Makani. I'm Luna. He's Jerry. You're Rell. Why is this so confusing?"

Jerry laughs and jumps down from the wall.

"It's not, Luna. The reef's scary when you're not from Lauele. Rell just wants to make sure the girls are safe."

"Didn't we just say so?" Luna says.

"Yes, but she needs to understand things for herself." Jerry jerks his head toward the tent. "If 'Ilima's here, Uncle Kahana is, too. Why don't you come in and meet him? He can show you the plans. It will just take a minute, and then we'll walk down to Piko Point."

"Piko Point?"

He points towards the girls again.

"Piko Point is at the end of the lava outcrop. From there I can show you where the surf tournament's held and tell you all about the surf camp."

From the ground, Jerry reaches up and places his hands along my waist. Without thinking I lean down and put my hands on his shoulders as he lifts me off the wall. On the ground, I have to look up a little to see his eyes. I know with just a little stretch, our lips would meet.

Cedar, cinnamon, cloves, and wintergreen mints.

Jerry clears his throat and smiles as he releases me, taking a half a step back.

"We are friends," sings Luna. "Friends, friends, friends! We are friends."

I turn toward him, but Luna's gone.

"What's that all about?" Jerry asks. "Why is he singing an old Cecilio & Kapono song?"

"Who knows," I say. "He's a little—"

"Strange?" Jerry raises an eyebrow.

I roll my eyes. "I was going to say quirky."

"You don't know the half of it," Jerry says, taking my hand. "C'mon. Let's check out the tent."

8

Inside the tent, a young woman with long hair piled on top of her head is smoothing tablecloths over a row of tables. Head down, she says, "Stack the brochures on the end, Luna. I want people to see the full list of auction items before they come in to bid." She looks up. "Oh, Jerry! I thought you were Luna."

"He's around here somewhere, Nalani. I just saw him," Jerry says.

"Luna!" Nalani shouts. "I need—"

"Already pau, Nalani!" says Luna's voice.

I turn, and a table that I swear wasn't there when I walked in is now next to the door and covered with artfully swirled stacks of brochures.

"What about the flowers?" Nalani says, placing her hands on her hips.

Like magic, a vase filled with purple bougainvillea appears.

"And pens!" Nalani says.

A woven basket of pens quivers next to the vase.

Nalani cracks her gum. "Why do I have to remind you buggahs about everything?"

"You're welcome," says Luna, but I can't tell if it's coming from under a table, behind the stacks of boxes, or outside the tent.

She cracks her gum again and smiles at us. "Who's your friend?"

Jerry says, "This is Rell Watanabe."

"Hi," I say and hold out my hand.

"As if." She ignores my hand and kisses my cheek. "Aloha, Rell. Strangers shake. 'Ohana honi—kiss."

"'Ohana? You mean family?"

"Don't look surprised. The word 'ohana existed long before *Lilo and Stitch*. And, yeah. We're second cousins on your mother's side. The last time I saw you, you were busy eating sand on Keikikai Beach."

"Ew!"

She shrugs. "It's what babies do. You don't remember coming to Lauele?"

"No."

Nalani puts her arm around my shoulders. "It was a long time ago. If your mother was still alive, I'm certain you would've been back many times. Let me get Uncle Kahana. He'll want to meet you."

"I have an Uncle Kahana?"

"Oh, honey! Everyone has an Uncle Kahana. There he is," she says. "E hui! Uncle Kahana! Someone to see you."

At the far end of the tent, in front of a massive stage, a slightly built elderly man in a faded t-shirt and worn board shorts turns toward us. He raises his brown arm and waves.

"Send 'em over, Nalani. It's too far for an old broke 'okole man to walk all the way over there."

Nalani gives me a little nudge, and Jerry and I thread our way through the tables.

Panic bubbles.

I have an Uncle Kahana.

People I don't know call me family.

My mother's family was from Lauele.

I give Jerry a side-glance.

I have to know.

"Are we related?" I whisper.

He pauses for a minute, considering. "Calabash cousins for sure. My great-great grandfather's aunty was hanai to your fifth cousin's mother, and she married my third cousin's nephew, so yeah, we're 'ohana."

Family.

My heart sinks.

"You know what calabash means, right?" Jerry says.

"No."

"It's an old Hawaiian idiom. Basically, it refers to all the people who make sure you never go hungry as well as the people you feed. It's less about sharing physical blood than sharing experiences and responsibilities."

I feel a sharp tug on the bottom of my shirt. When I reach back, I feel Luna's thick hand squeeze mine.

"Don't worry," he whispers. "Calabash cousins can date."

I spin around, but all I see is the edge of a tablecloth settling against the floor.

"Did you say something?" Jerry asks.

"Me? No."

I hear a giggle, and then Luna's voice sings, "Friends, friends, friends."

"It's just Luna singing again," I say.

"Luna. What a pest!" Jerry says.

"So, we're calabash cousins, but not blood."

"Right," he says.

Calabash. The butterflies settle. It might not make a difference to him, but it does to me.

Wait a minute.

I touch his arm. "Is that why you lent me your truck?"

Jerry shakes his head. "Of course not. I didn't know you were 'ohana until I saw Luna talking with you. One of his quirks is he only talks with family."

"But I'd never met him before. How could he possibly know me?"

Jerry shrugs. "I don't know. But no one outside of family ever sees him or his crew."

Luna giggles again. From somewhere around my knees, he sing-songs, "First comes love, then comes marriage, then comes Rell with a—"

I smack the tabletop.

"Cockroach?" Jerry asks. "They get pretty big in Hawaii."

"It's nothing."

Luna giggles again.

Imp.

"Close," says a voice in my ear, "but not quite."

9

It doesn't take us long to reach the far end of the tent where Uncle Kahana is standing next to a table with an architect's model.

"Uncle Kahana, this is—"

"Rell Watanabe." He leans over and kisses my cheek. "You look like your mother."

It's so unexpected that I have to catch my breath.

"You knew my mother?"

"Of course. And your father. And your grand-parents—"

"Yeah, Uncle Kahana is real old," says Jerry.

Uncle Kahana narrows his eyes. "Don't you have cars to park?"

"Nope."

"You sure? I hear you college boys are good at that."

"The best! We learned from old futs like you."

Uncle Kahana snorts and wags his finger. "One of these days, Jerry, if you're lucky, you'll get to be as old as me."

"I hope so, Uncle, I hope so."

"But for now, Jerry, let me show Rell the surf camp. It's because of Watanabe Global that it's possible." Uncle Kahana motions for me to come closer. "This is why we're here."

The model shows six cabins connected by paved trails with ramps and handrails. Near the parking lot are outdoor showers, racks for storing surfboards, and a covered pavilion with cooking facilities. Uncle Kahana opens one of the cabins like a dollhouse.

"Four beds in each cabin's main room with a separate space for aides or camp counselors. No bunk beds. Everything's extra-wide for wheelchairs, and the bathrooms have rails and chairs in the showers. The goal is to allow campers to live as independently as possible."

"You should see the zip lines and towers. Awesome," Jerry says.

"That's not until Phase Two, when we add the obstacle courses for strength and agility training." Uncle Kahana shoots me a glance. "You know about the tournament?"

I shake my head. "I don't know anything. Tell me."

"When the Abilities Surf Tournament went international and got corporate sponsorship, Jay and Nili-boy came up with the idea to add a summer surfing camp. When they started, the whole thing was sponsored by Get Wet Prosthetics and some grants, but frankly they can't do it without the support of businesses like Watanabe Global. This camp is going to be life changing."

I run a finger over a cabin. "It's a camp for kids who want to become pro surfers?"

Uncle Kahana's head snaps toward me. He frowns and opens his mouth, but doesn't speak. I look up from the model and catch his eyes. He reads something in my face and softens.

"The camp is for more than just kids, Rell. Adults, too."

"But the goal is to win the competition, right? It's a surf tournament."

Uncle Kahana chuckles quietly. "No. The goal is to heal. When bodies, minds, hearts, and souls are healed, they have a desire to test themselves. Competition is the natural result, that's all. You've been to Piko Point?"

Jerry says, "Not yet. She just got off the plane this morning."

"Take her, Jerry. Tell her. It will all make sense then." He cocks an eyebrow at me. "You surf?"

I smile and echo Jerry. "Not yet."

He pats my arm. "No worries! With a name like Rell, you'll be a natural."

10

At the edge of the sand near the showers, Jerry stops. He steps out of his shoes and pulls off his socks.

"No shoes," he says. "Only tourists walk on beaches in shoes."

"We're supposed to carry them?"

He takes my shoes from me and sets them next to his on top of the short rock wall.

"You want me to leave my shoes here? Are you nuts? I only have one other pair. Someone will steal them."

He looks at me, amused. "This is Lauele. Nobody'll bother them. Promise."

I step off the walkway and onto the sand. It's warm on the top and cooler underneath as it squishes between my toes. There's a light breeze coming off the ocean. It's not enough to chop the water, just enough to keep things from getting too hot. At Keikikai Beach, the water is bathtub calm and clear as glass. A little ways down the beach, a young mother is splashing with her toddler, but other than them, the beach is empty.

"Where is everyone?"

He cuffs my shoulder. "It's Friday afternoon. Most people in paradise work for a living."

"I mean, where are the girls?" Panic rises. "I don't see them."

Jerry shades his eyes. "There. Walking out to Piko Point. They're on the Nalupuki side."

I follow his arm to the lava outcrop stretching out to sea. On the far side I see waves splash as they hit the rocks. This side is calm. The other is wild. I have a vision of the girls tumbling into the rough water, followed by my head on Regina's wall.

I shift my weight and run.

"Rell! Wait!"

At the start of the rocks, Jerry catches my arm, forcing me to stop.

"Slow down. Makani's with them, remember? They're just exploring."

"I have to get out there."

"Okay, but don't run. You're barefoot, remember? Parts of the reef are slippery. Other spots are sharp. Let's go slow. Step where I step."

His hand travels down my arm to grab my hand.

"We have to wade just a bit to get to the first rock. It won't get higher than your knees, promise. But keep your eye on the water. You never want to turn your back to the ocean."

I tell myself it's the shock of the water that makes me squirm and not the feeling of holding a boy's hand.

Good grief.

Maybe an all-girls prep school isn't everything it's cracked up to be.

We step out of the ocean and onto the lava. It's rough and rippled like water and dotted with pockets of salt, but it feels warm under my toes.

I raise a hand to my eyes and peer out toward the point. The girls are sitting down near a big saltwater pool, watching something in the water. 'Ilima is sitting a few yards away, chewing her tail.

"It's easy," Jerry says. "But watch where you step. It's low tide, so there might be some wana exposed."

"What's that?"

"It looks like a black ball of spikes. It's a sea urchin. Nothing to worry about, but you really don't want to step on one."

"It's like a sea cactus?"

Jerry snorts. "Good one. Just don't let them hear you say that."

"Wana are sensitive?"

His eyes twinkle. "Totally!"

When we get near the girls, I hear them arguing.

Ana says, "It's a killer snake."

"You're lying," Zel says.

"I saw a video about it. One bite from a sea snake, and you're dead before you get back to shore."

"Nuh-uh."

"Put your foot in the water and wave it around if you don't believe me."

"You do it."

"Hi girls," I say.

Ana looks up. "Let's make Rell do it."

"Yeah. Rell, put your foot in the water."

"So a sea snake can bite it? That's not very nice."

Ana's eyes flit to Zel. "There's no snake," she says.

"We just want to know how cold the water is," Zel says.

Jerry squats down next to the girls. "Put your own hand in the water. Rell can't tell you if it's cold."

"Who're you?" Ana asks.

I say, "This is Jerry."

"Is he your boyfriend?" Zel asks.

I shoot Jerry a look.

Why? Why do I do this? He's not my boyfriend. I don't have to check with him to see if he agrees.

"No," I say evenly. "But he is my friend. We drove to the beach in his truck."

"Ugh. That old thing? You need a better truck," says Zel.

"Yeah, your truck smells like seaweed."

"And stale burritos."

My face turns purple.

Let a wave take me now.

Please.

I can't look at Jerry.

The girls are beyond rude.

Jerry throws his head back and laughs.

"Of course it smells like seaweed and burritos. It's a surf truck."

Zel and Ana's eyes bug out of their heads.

"Are you crazy?" Ana says.

"Or just weird?" Zel says as she stands.

She moves toward a rock the size and shape of a basketball perched near the edge of the biggest tide pool.

"Careful!" Jerry says. "That rock is called Pohaku. It's part of an ancient fishing shrine. Be respectful, and don't get too close."

"What?"

"Stay away from that rock," Jerry says. "It's not something you touch or play with."

"Come on, Ana," says Zel. "Let's leave the love birds alone."

"Yeah, love birds." Ana rises and makes kissy noises as she walks over to another tide pool. "Ooo! A crab! Let's catch it!"

Jerry stands. "Charming. Your sisters?"

I sigh. "Stepsisters."

"Wicked little demons, aren't they?"

"I don't really know. I haven't seen them in years. But you're probably right."

The water in the saltwater pool is deep, but I can see all the way to the bottom and through a large archway that leads to black water.

"Is there a sea snake?"

He shrugs. "It's possible, but highly unlikely. Sea snakes are really rare in Hawaiian waters. I've never seen one. It was probably an eel."

I bend down and run my fingers along the surface of the water. "It's colder out here than near the shore."

"Right off the point is deep water. There's a channel between us and the other side. That's what makes Nalupuki a great surfing beach."

Beneath my fingers, the water stirs. A thin rope peeks from a crevasse, then shoots out to wind between my fingers. I'm too surprised to jerk my hand away.

"What's that?"

Jerry gasps. "It's a baby snowflake eel. They're usually really shy. I've never seen one do this. It's like he's happy to see you."

More fish rise from the bottom and head to the surface. I see yellow tangs and purple damsel fish, striped sergeant majors, and others I don't recognize. I pull my hand out of the water.

"They must think I have food," I say. "Do people come out here and feed them?"

The look on Jerry's face is odd. It rolls through different expressions until it lands on something between sheepish and puzzled.

"Nobody I know," he says.

I stand and look at the strip of sand off to the right. Just past it is the hillside from the architect's model.

"That's where the surf camp is going?"

Jerry nods. "Yeah. That's Kaulupali land over there. Your family owns a few acres just above it. Uncle Kahana is gifting some of his Kaulupali land to Jay's foundation to use for the surf camp. Come out to the very edge of the lava with me, and I'll tell you the whole story."

"There's a mystery?" I tease. "A deep, dark secret?"

But when Jerry reaches for my hand to help me over a slippery patch, I see the pain in his eyes.

"There's a reason for the surf tournament and the camp." He sweeps his arm out over the bay.

"It all began here during our freshman year of high school."

Out at the very edge of the lava outcrop, the waves splash against the rocks, sending a fine mist toward us. In the water just off the point, a guy on a green surfboard and a girl on a cream one wait for the next set. The guy waves at Jerry.

"Santos!" he shouts. "Where's your board?"

"Home," Jerry says.

"Brah! Better hurry. Kids will be out of school soon," calls the girl.

"Can't," Jerry says.

"You snooze, you lose! The waves wait for no one," says the guy.

Like magic, a gentle swell forms off the point. The surfers swing their legs onto their boards and paddle into position where the wave suddenly builds four feet higher.

"Chee-hoo!" the guy calls.

"Laters, Jerry!" says the girl.

Jerry's eyes are on the surfers as they head to shore.

"You surf here a lot?"

He nods, but doesn't look at me. "From the time we could walk, we were in the ocean. Like I said, the International Abilities Surf Tournament, Get Wet, the surf camp—it all begins here."

He tugs my hand until our shoulders touch.

"Our freshman year, Jay Westin and I were competing in a surf tournament. Jay was the favorite." His lips twist wryly. "In those days, Jay was always the favorite. When the heat started, we all raced from the beach, paddling to get to the sweet spot just there," he points, "right where those surfers were. The waves were bigger that day. We were jockeying for position when someone yelled, 'Fin!'"

I look back to the beach and shiver.

It's so far.

"But it was just a dolphin, right?"

"No. Sharks. I saw them."

"Them?"

"Two. One the size of Jaws and the other his littler brother. Jay was out farther than the rest of us. From Piko Point, the shark fins made a beeline to him and disappeared."

"They left?"

Jerry shakes his head. "They dove. Sharks ambush. The biggest one rocketed from the bottom and came up underneath Jay's board, knocking him off and into the water. I saw the other one circling below."

I squeeze his hand. I have no words.

"When Jay came up for air, he shouted at us to go—to head back to shore."

"But you didn't."

"I couldn't. I knew he'd never leave me. I heard sirens and jet skis start up on the beach. I tried to paddle toward Jay. I thought if I could get him up on my board, we'd be okay. I knew help was coming, but before I could get there— "

He swallows and presses his lips tight, the horror of that day as fresh as a minute before him.

"The smaller shark bit Jay."

"You saw that?"

"Yeah. In all its technicolor glory. Red blood in blue water looks purple. Seafoam turns pink. Bone is whiter than white." Jerry reaches down and touches his shin a few inches above his ankle. "It ate his foot."

"My—"

I can't even say it.

Jerry tugs my hand until I look him in the eye.

"Jay lost his foot, but more importantly, he lost himself that day. Before the attack, being in the ocean was like breathing to him. People think losing a limb is about what someone can or can't do, but that's the smallest part of it."

"Jay Westin. You said he started Get Wet Prosthetics?"

Jerry nods. "That came later. After it happened, Jay filled his empty surfing space with hate. It took a lot of time, but the ocean eventually healed him—body, mind, heart, and soul. He figured out how to surf again. To forgive himself."

"Himself?"

"You sound surprised."

"But it's the shark who took his foot."

"It's complicated." Jerry rubs his face. "Anyway, Jay

and his cousin Nili-boy started Get Wet Prosthetics to help others reconnect with the lives they were meant to live." He gestured toward the beach. "This camp is the next step. Watanabe Global is doing a lot of good by supporting the auction. That's one reason why I helped you."

"One?"

Jerry presses his shoulder against mine. "Don't push it," he says.

I watch the surfers pull out of the wave and head back out.

"After what you saw, you still surf?"

"Every day I can. Rain or shine, big waves or glass."

I look at the waves crashing against the lava and think about pink foam and white bone.

"I'd never get in the water again."

"You only say that because you've never surfed."

"What about sharks? They're still out there."

Jerry gives me a side-glance. "We worked it out. It's all cool now."

"What—"

Bark, bark, bark, BARK, BARKBARKBARK!

We whirl around in time to see the girls rocking the round stone perched on the edge of the biggest tide pool. 'Ilima's dancing around them, her jaws snapping like a shark.

BARKBARKBARK.

"Come on, Ana! One more push, and we'll get it in the water!"

"No!" shouts Jerry as he lurches toward them. He slips on the lava and falls to his knees. "Stop it! You don't know what you're doing!"

The stone starts to tip.

"Girls," I say as I scramble around Jerry.

'Ilima leaps and bites one of Ana's ruffles, tugging the back of her suit off her hips.

"Eeee!" Ana shrieks. "I'm being attacked!"

The stone tumbles.

Zel pumps her fist. "Yes!"

'Ilima releases Ana's suit and rushes to the edge of

the tide pool. As the stone sinks to the bottom, big silver bubbles rise like jellyfish and pop at the surface. 'Ilima collapses on the lava, raises her head, and howls.

"Stupid dog," Zel says, marching over. "Nobody bites my sister but me!"

She swings her foot, kicking 'Ilima squarely in the ribs.

'Ilima's howl turns into a yelp. She leaps to her feet, saltwater dripping off her chest. Pinning her ears back, she growls.

"Zel! Ana! Don't move!" I say.

"That dog pantsed me!" Ana says, pulling her suit up over her butt. "Kick it again, Zel!"

"Ana, are you hurt? Let me see."

I spin her around, but she covers her backside with both hands.

"Don't! You're as pervy as the dog."

There's not a mark on her.

Zel draws back her foot again. "Don't you growl at me, crazy dog. I'll kick you again."

"No, you won't!" I grab each of them by the arm. "Stop this right now!"

It's not until I turn back to Jerry that I see the tears in his eyes. He's kneeling at the edge of the pool, staring at the bottom in shock.

"Jerry?"

No response.

"Jerry, your knee is bleeding. Are you okay?"

At the sight of blood, the girls still.

He raises his eyes from the water and looks at the girls. "Why?" Tears spill down his cheeks. "That was a sacred 'aumakua stone. A guardian of this place for hundreds of years. People come here to pray, to meditate, to leave offerings. I told you it's an ancient shrine. I told you to leave it alone."

Zel scrunches up her face. "It's just a stupid rock."

Ana says, "Yeah. If it's so important, why did people leave it here?"

'Ilima lowers her head and growls deeper.

Jerry stands and pulls his shirt over his head, tossing it on the ground. The sunlight glistens on his surfer's broad shoulders and trim waist.

"Go," he says. "Get them out of my sight."

His hands move to his belt.

Ana pulls her arm out of my grasp.

"You're not the boss of us," she says.

Jerry unbuckles his belt and moves to the top button of his cargo shorts. "Leave before I'm tempted to use my belt to do more than hold up my pants."

"I'm tell—ow!" Ana says when I grab her by the ear.

"You can't—ow, ow, ow!" chants Zel.

I twist their ears a little harder.

"I'm not your nanny. I'm your big sister and that does make me the boss of you! We're going home. Now."

Ana and Zel try to plant their feet, but I twist relentlessly and force them to stumble back to the beach.

I hear a splash and look over my shoulder. Jerry's pants are on the ground near the big saltwater pool. His feet sink below the surface.

After what the girls did, he'll never speak to me again.

Goodbye, Jerry's feet.

Zel realizes I'm distracted and tries to pull away, but I grip harder.

"Stop it, Rell! You're hurting me!"

"Good."

At the rock wall near the showers, I let go of the girls long enough to grab my shoes.

Jerry's shoes.

I run my fingers over them.

Goodbye, Jerry's shoes.

It's been real.

I turn on the shower and rinse my feet.

"Into the water," I say.

"No."

"It's too cold."

"We'll shower at home."

"You're not getting sand in the car and making more work for Jerry. Rinse."

"No."

Oh, yes. Yes, you will.

I grab ruffles.

"Let go!"

I twist for a better grip.

"Hey!"

"Rinse the sand off your feet or I'll dunk your whole body under the spray," I say.

"You can't make us."

"You're not the boss!"

I yank, pulling their legs into the spray.

"Cold, cold, cold!" they shriek.

"Good," I say.

"Ha! Fooled you. It's not that bad."

"Yeah, we wanted to anyway!"

"Let's get really wet and soak the car!"

"Yeah! Water's way worse than sand."

Out the corner of my eye, I spot 'Ilima limping around the showers and slinking behind the trash cans.

She's following us.

That can't be good.

"Let's go," I say.

'Ilima trails us all the way past the event tent and across the street to the rental car. I unlock it and push Zel toward the backseat.

"It's too small," she whines.

"Complain to your mother."

"It's too hot," Ana says.

"Get in."

"I want to sit up front."

"No, I want to," Zel says.

I grit my teeth. "You both get in the back right this minute or so help me, I'll leave, and you can walk."

"I hate you!" Ana says.

"Right back at ya," I say.

"I'm telling Mom," Zel says. "She'll punish you for being mean to us."

I count to three, then slide the driver's seat all the way forward. "Get in."

They grumble, but finally climb in. When I get in, I feel their knees and feet pushing against my back.

They want to be that way? Fine.

I turn all the air conditioning vents toward me and start the engine.

"Hey! What about us?"

"Can we put the top down? It's hot."

"No. Be quiet."

"I want a drink."

"Me, too."

"Let's go in the store."

"No," I say.

"Come on, Rell. Buy us a drink."

"It's hot, and we're thirsty."

I adjust the mirrors. "You can get one at the house."

"You're so mean, Rell."

"Mom was right about you."

When I put the car in reverse, 'Ilima steps out of shadows to watch us leave. I roll down my window.

"I'm sorry," I tell her. "I hope your ribs are okay. I won't let them hurt you again."

"What's Rell saying?"

"She's apologizing to the dog!"

"That dog attacked me!"

"It should be put down!"

"She's crazy. I can't believe Mom sent us with her."

'Ilima locks eyes with me.

My eyes dim like I'm going to faint. I take a deep breath and try to shake the ringing out of my ears.

I smell sandalwood and lemonade.

'Ilima tips her head to the side and chuffs.

The taste of lemons fills my mouth, sweet and sour and a little salty, just the way Mama used to make it.

In an instant, I'm three years old again, running through the backyard sprinklers. Mama says, "Rell! Time for lunch, sweetheart."

Mama?

"What are we waiting for?" Ana whines.

"It's so hot!"
I swallow, and the memory's gone.
When I look back, 'Ilima isn't there.
"Mom is so going to hear about this," says Zel.
"Uh-huh," says Ana.

I'm so angry that I don't consider parking on the street when I get to the estate and pull all the way to the back of the house. I grab my purse from the seat next to me, throw the keys inside, and hold the door open for the girls. They climb out acting stiff and sore, like I forced them to ride twisted like pretzels in a box. A door opens, and Regina stalks out.

"My precious," she says, throwing her arms wide.

"Mommy!" the twins shout and rush to her, crocodile tears falling like rain.

"My lambkins! What's wrong? Are you hurt?"

"Mommy, Rell yelled at us."

Regina's jaw clenches as her eye starts to twitch. "I'm sure it was just a misunderstanding. Rell knows better than to yell at you."

"Regina—"

"And Mommy, we were thirsty, but she refused to let us drink!"

"What! In this heat?" Regina pulls the girls close.

"That's cruel, Rell, even for someone as thoughtless and uncaring as you."

"She made us ride in the back without air conditioning!"

"That's not all! She twisted our ears! Look!" Ana flips back her hair.

Regina looks at Ana's ear, then Zel's.

"Oh, my babies! Your ears are all red and swollen!"

"Regina—"

Regina rises to her full height and squares her shoulders. "I am so disappointed in you, Rell. I wish I could say I was shocked, but I'm not."

"The girls pushed—"

She holds up her hand. "I don't want to hear it. Clearly, this is my fault. I thought if you spent some time with your sisters, you'd love them as much as they love you. I thought you'd decide you missed us and would want to be part of the family again. But I see my hopes were misplaced. Your father was right about you."

Her words stop me cold.

Victory shines behind her eyes. She's daring me to ask.

I won't give her the satisfaction.

It's a stare-down until one of us blinks.

She holds out her hand. "Keys," she says.

I blink.

"What?"

She wiggles her fingers. "Give me your keys. After the way you've behaved, you're not going anywhere."

"But the auction—"

"I don't want you anywhere near the auction.

You've proven you can't be trusted. You'll spend the night in your room."

"I—"

Faster than a snake, Zel reaches out and tugs my purse off my shoulder.

"Got it, Mommy! Her keys are inside."

"Give that back!" I reach to swipe it from her, but Regina sweeps Zel protectively behind her.

"Don't you touch her. You've done enough damage."

Zel unzips my purse and pulls out my phone. "We got her cell, too!" she crows.

"Give me Rell's phone," says Ana.

"Why?"

"I want to send text messages to her friends."

"She doesn't have any friends," says Zel, pushing buttons. "Oh, man! Her phone's locked! We can't text from it."

"Let's throw it in the toilet!"

"Yeah!"

"Come back here," I say and move towards the door. Regina blocks me.

"Run along and get ready, dears."

"But we don't want to go to the auction."

"Bor-ring!"

Regina pats their heads. "You're not going to the auction, sillies. That's for grownups. I've arranged for all the good girls to spend the night at the fabulous Princess Party at Disney's Aulani Resort."

"Rell's not a grownup," Zel says.

"She's not a good girl either," snickers Ana. "At the party, I'm going to be Jasmine."

"No, I am!"

"Too late. I called it."

"You're Olaf!"

"Olaf isn't a princess!"

The girls bicker all the way into the house.

They still have my phone!

I better not find it in the toilet.

Regina says, "We need to talk."

I scowl. "I've nothing to say to you."

"Then listen." She steps close, so close I can see the makeup spackled under her eyes. "We can do things the easy way or the hard way. It doesn't matter to me. If you want to keep going to that fancy school, you'll do what I say. Otherwise, I'll cut your funding, and you'll be out on the street."

"Why can't I go to the auction?"

"Because I said so. This deal is bigger than you know. You've proven that you can't handle taking two little girls to the beach. There's no way I'm letting you near something this important."

"Funding a surf camp for disabled people is big? That makes no sense, Regina. What's your angle?"

"No imagination. That's what your father said about you. Rell wears her heart on her sleeve, he said. There's no way she could ever play poker."

"Regina—"

"Get your things. I'll show you to your room. In the morning you can drive yourself to the airport."

Oh, no.

My bag.

In my mind, I clearly see it in the back of Jerry's truck.

She sees the look on my face. Her eyes widen like it's *her* birthday.

"You don't have it?"

"It's—I think I left it in the back of the truck."

"You have no clothes."

"No."

Regina throws her head back and cackles. "No car, no phone, no clothes! How utterly perfect. There's no way for you to go now."

On my way to a tiny room just off the kitchen, I discover the laundry room. After Regina and her entourage leave, I toss my clothes in the washer and take a long, hot shower. Wrapped in a fluffy towel, with no one else around, I pour myself a glass of guava juice, make a peanut butter sandwich, and scrounge up a bag of chips. Shivering, I take them outside to sit in the twilight while my clothes dry.

Damp hair hanging down my back, I sit on a chaise lounge on the patio and sigh. Even though the sun has gone down, it's far warmer outside than in the house. Regina must have the air conditioning cranked. I could almost see my breath when I got out of the shower.

My dinner sits next to me on a small side table.

I need to eat. That iffy breakfast burrito on the plane was hours ago.

I take a bite of sandwich, but I can't swallow past the lump in my throat.

Accentuate the positive, Rell. Don't let Regina get you down.

Bright side: At least I'll have clean clothes for the plane ride home.

Clean clothes. Big whoop.

I force the down the bite of sandwich and wipe my eyes on a corner of the towel. Time to suck it up. Only babies cry. Big girls pull up their panties and problem solve.

Even if their panties are still in the dryer.

Identifying the problems is always the first step in dealing with Regina.

Problem one: car keys. I'll search the house. I doubt Regina took them with her.

Problem two: my phone. There's got to be a landline for the house. Find it and call Jerry.

Problem three: Jerry's number. I need my purse. It has Jerry's business card.

Problem four: find a phone book or computer. Call the rental company. Somebody there can give me Jerry's cell.

Call his work?

Gee, Rell, that's not stalkerish at all.

Oh, Jerry.

What would I even say? Sorry my wicked stepsisters pushed your special rock into the ocean? Hope you were able to get it out?

Unbelievable.

I can't forget the look on his face.

I should've stayed and helped him instead of running away like an idiot.

He'll wonder why I'm not at the party.

He'll think I'm mad at him or something.

Who am I kidding? He'll be relieved I'm not there.

I look at my sandwich and soggy chips and wrinkle my nose. *I bet they're having dinner now. Luau food like roast pork and fresh pineapple.*

Bright side: peanut butter's okay. A little sticky. Filling. The bread's fresh.

Hey, another one: The surf camp will be built. That's a good thing, right?

But it makes no sense. Why would Regina care about a surf camp? There's no margin in it.

Jerry—

Stop it. Just stop it.

A guy like that probably has a girlfriend. The way Luna talked, probably several *friends.*

Cedar, cinnamon, cloves, and wintergreen mints.

The sunlight on his bare shoulders when he took off his shirt.

Should've kissed him when I had the chance.

Just one dance at the party. Is that so much to wish for? It's my birthday, for crying out loud.

I'm not going to cry.

Not going to.

Dang it!

Through the tears, I see a star peeking over the mountain top.

The first star.

No candles on my birthday cake. Heck, no birthday cake! I'm not wasting this chance.

"Starlight, star bright; first star I see tonight; I wish I may; I wish I might; have the wish I wish tonight."

I close my eyes and wish.

"Woof."

I whip open my eyes. In the shadows on the far side of the patio is a yellow dog.

"'Ilima?"

She limps towards me until she is standing in a pool of moonlight. I rise from my chair and lean forward, one hand clutching my towel, the other outstretched.

"Hey, girl. What're you doing here? That's a long walk from the beach. How're your ribs?"

She sits and cocks her head at me. Her tongue drops out of her mouth as she pants.

"Thirsty? Be right back."

In the kitchen I fill a bowl full of cool water and bring it out to the patio.

I set it next to her. "Here you go."

She glances at it, then bats it away with her paw.

"You don't want it?"

Her eyes lock like laser beams on my sandwich. She smacks her lips.

"Sandwiches aren't for dogs."

She whines and lies down, resting her head on her paws. Her eyes never leave my sandwich.

"Really? You like peanut butter?"

"Woof!" She sits up, ears forward.

I shrug. "Okay."

I tear off a chunk and toss it to her.

She catches it mid-air and gulps it whole.

"Careful! You keep eating like that, you'll choke."

Her ears droop as her body shakes, quivering in the moonlight. The air fills with the scent of sandalwood and lemons. Sparkles of silver light cascade down her body like glitter as she bows her head. I hear chanting or drums—a rhythmic beating that pulses like ocean waves against the shore. A gust of wind swirls around the patio, blowing the bag of chips to the ground.

"'Ilima?"

The high, clear note of a conch shell echoes against the house, a wall of sound so loud I cover my ears.

"'Ilima, what's going on?" I shout. "We better get inside."

Her limbs and torso elongate as she rises.

Before me stands a beautiful Hawaiian woman.

"'I—'I—'Ilima?"

"Woof," she says.

I step back and almost trip over my own feet. My heart is pounding. I can't get enough air to breathe, let alone scream.

The woman laughs, and it is the sound of wind chimes and beach glass. "Relax," she says, rolling her shoulders and neck. "I'm just playing with you." She touches her ribs and grimaces. "Although I could've done without the kick in the ribs. What's the matter with those two? Are they retarded?"

Reflexively, I say, "Don't say retarded. People aren't retarded."

She smiles without showing her teeth. "My mistake. It's tough to keep up with your human terms; they change so often. What should I say?"

"Intellectually disabled or differently abled."

This conversation is surreal. I shake my head to clear it, but the woman is still there.

"Are they?" she says.

I blink. "What?"

"Intellectually differently abled?" she says.

"No." I cock my head to the side. "At least I don't think so."

"Ah. Just plain mean, then. Good. That makes this easier." She stares at the rest of the sandwich still in my hand. "You going to finish that?"

"Uh, no. Knock yourself out," I say as I hand it to her.

Her fingers brush mine.

Oh, man. She's real.

'Ilima the woman takes dainty bites, but finishes the sandwich as fast as a dog.

"Oh, that's better," she says. "Changing form always makes me hungry!" She points to the glass of guava juice. "May I?"

"Be my guest."

Like I'm going to say no.

She drains the drink in one great swallow. "Umm, that's good," she says.

She sees me watching her.

She deliberately raises the empty glass to her lips.

She raises an eyebrow.

And takes a bite.

Glass crumbles and falls to the ground.

What the?

She chews.

Crunch, crunch, crunch.

She smiles, this time showing her teeth. There are little bits of glass clinging to her lips.

The world starts to dim. There's a buzz, buzz, buzzing in my ears.

This time I really do faint.

When I come to, I'm lying on the chaise lounge. 'Ilima is holding out a glass of water.

"Don't worry. It's a new one from the kitchen. I didn't even lick it."

I sit up too fast. The blood rushes from my head.

Don't faint. Don't faint.

It's all over if I faint.

'Ilima puts a hand on her hip and waves the glass near my face.

"Take it. Drink. Trust me. It's all going to be okay. I promise."

The water is cold against my tongue as I gulp it. When it hits my stomach, I feel more awake.

"Better?"

I nod.

"Good." She holds out her hand and pulls me to my feet. The towel starts to fall, but I catch it and wrap it tighter against my chest.

"Jerry, huh?" She circles behind me. "A girl could do a lot worse."

She snorts bitterly. "Many have."

She prods my back.

"Tall, but not too tall. Slender, almost willowy."

She runs her fingers through my hair.

"Good girl," she says with a snicker.

Is she petting *me?*

I bite my lip.

Don't lose it, Rell. Don't laugh.

"Nice hair. You've given me a lot to work with."

"Work how? What're you going to do with me?"

"Give you a birthday present, of course. What did you think was going to happen?"

"I have no idea."

She faces me again. "Look," she says, holding up a mirror.

"Where did—"

But then I see the girl in the mirror, and it doesn't matter where the mirror came from.

"That can't be me!" I say.

'Ilima smirks. "Of course it is."

"It can't be."

"How do you know? Have you ever seen the real you?"

It's me, but a me I've never seen before.

I'm wearing a silk floral shift tied over my shoulder. My hair is swept high and to the side with cascading curls. The smell of the gardenias in my hair mixes with the twisted lei of tiny white flowers around my neck.

I reach up to touch them.

"Pikake," she says. "A kind of jasmine. Don't touch or they'll brown."

My makeup is subtle. Just a few sweeps of mascara on my eyelashes, a kiss of blush along my cheekbones, and a light coral lip stain. My skin looks radiant. Dangling from my ears are simple gold drops in the shape of the flowers in my lei. On my feet are thin leather flip flops that show off my newly manicured toes. A glance at my fingers shows the same finishing touch.

Oh, no.

I reach down and run fingers over my shins.

Smooth as a baby's bottom.

'Ilima smirks. "Pits, too. I'm guessing your razor is in your bag."

"How—"

"Granted, Jerry probably would have preferred you in the towel, but let's not throw ourselves at him anymore that we already have, shall we?"

"Why—"

"So you can go to the party and dance with your beau. That's what you wanted, right?"

I turn sideways in the mirror. "But this—"

"You were expecting a poufy blue dress and impractical heels? Mainlanders," she scoffs. "No sense of style."

"How—"

She lowers the mirror and tsks. "Good grief, child. Speak in complete sentences. I know you can."

She raises the mirror again, holding it in front of me like a wish.

"See? Perfect. Jerry is waiting. You want to go or not?"

I swallow.

"Yes."

"Good."

"But I don't have my car keys—"

A car pulls into the driveway and beeps its horn.

"Gecko," she says. "Hawaii's version of Uber or Lyft. Much better than your Mini Cooper pumpkin coach, even if we had the keys. Come along, Rell. We don't have all night."

As I get in the car, the driver doesn't say a word, just twitches nervously. In the rearview mirror I see that his eyes are slit like a reptile's. He sees me watching and quickly slips on a pair of dark glasses. His fingertips are odd, too big and puffy for his hands. Before I can look further, 'Ilima pushes the door closed and stands outside the car twiddling a finger at me. I roll down the window.

"Here's the deal: The car and driver will be waiting for you as soon as you step back into the parking lot. No need to call. The driver will only bring you back here, so don't bother trying to get to the airport or someplace crazy like that. You kiss that boy, the one you wished on, the car won't come. In fact, if you kiss him, you'll go back to standing in a towel with wet hair dripping down your back. Transitions are funny. The towel may shrink a little, too, so keep that in mind."

I reach through the open window and touch her arm. "Thank you, 'Ilima. It's a wish come true."

She lifts my hand off her arm and gives it a little

squeeze. "I'm not a fairy godmother, Rell. I don't grant wishes; I pay my debts. That's all this is."

"Who are you?"

"Don't look a gift horse in the mouth." She sees the look on my face and softens. "It's your birthday, Rell. Go have fun."

The tent at Keikikai Beach glows like a candle. As we pull up, I hear live music; guitars and ukuleles strum as a velvety voice caresses a melody filled with Hawaiian vowels. The driver takes me all the way to edge of the red carpet where a perky young man in a blue aloha shirt opens my door and presents me with his hand.

"Aloha!" he says. "Do you need parking assistance?"

"Um," I mumble as I exit the car.

"No," croaks the driver.

As soon as I'm standing on the edge of the carpet, the driver hits the gas. The valet barely has time to get the door closed.

"Whoa!" yells the valet. "Where's the fire?" He turns to me. "Are you okay?"

I take a deep breath. "Yes. Thank you."

"That guy's crazy. Do you know him?"

"No. He's a hired driver."

He pulls out a cell phone. "Which company?"

"Gecko."

"Gecko? Never heard of them." He raises an eyebrow. "You sure he's legit?"

I stifle a laugh. "He was provided by my—"

By my *what*? My dog? I shudder. 'Ilima's not my dog. Definitely not my fairy godmother, either. My gift horse? I bite my lip to keep from laughing.

The valet's eyebrow goes higher.

I'm taking too long to answer.

I cover my hesitation with a cough.

"Oh, excuse me. Sorry, got a frog in my throat. The driver was sent by my, um, *benefactor*. He came highly recommended."

The valet holds out his phone. "You should report him. There's no excuse for that."

"I will."

Although I don't think a dog who isn't a dog is going to care very much.

The valet wiggles his phone.

Oh, no. He's still waiting for me to make the call.

"Thanks, but I'll call later," I say. "No need to spoil the evening."

He slips his phone back into his pocket and holds out a hand. "Your invitation, miss?"

Invitation?

Crap.

I'm not carrying a purse. I run my hands down my sides, but the shift has no pockets. I hold out my empty hands, give a weak smile, and shrug.

His eyes do a quick sweep from head to toe, assessing. He must like what he sees, because he smiles and says, "It's okay. Just tell me your name so I can have it announced."

Double crap!

"That's not necessary," I stammer. I try to step past him, but he takes a step sideways, forcing me to stay on the edge of the red carpet.

"I know it sounds silly, but it's an old-fashioned tradition the organizers are insisting on."

This is the last thing I need.

"I don't want to bother everyone," I say. "After all, I'm late. The event has already started."

"It's not a bother. Look, other people are waiting to be announced."

I peek around him and see a short queue of guests lined up at the top of the red carpet. At the archway leading into the tent stands a seven foot mountain of a man in silver brocade livery. Two teenage boys in loincloths block the doorway with crossed wooden staffs topped with white cloth balls.

At the giant's nod, a couple hands a gilt-edged card to him. He regards it for a second, then nods again. The couple steps forward, the staffs are uncrossed and whisked aside, and another man in a loincloth and a short feathered cape softly blows on a conch shell. As the echo dies, the giant announces the couple's names and ushers them in. Once the couple enters the tent, the wooden staffs are crossed again, and the whole thing starts over.

I sigh.

Only Regina would insist on something so pompous and ridiculous.

Inside the tent, nobody seems to be paying much

attention to the guests' arrivals. The music doesn't pause, and I can see people talking as they wander between the tables filled with auction items.

Maybe it's no big deal. Even if he announces me, it's unlikely Regina will hear it.

"Your name, miss," the valet prods. "Tell me quick, and it will be over before you know it."

Fine. Here goes nothing.

"I'm Rell," I say. "Rell Watanabe."

The valet jumps back. "Rell Watanabe! I'm so sorry, Ms. Watanabe! Your driver should've brought you to the special VIP entrance! Let's get you right to the front!"

He gestures frantically to the giant. VIP, he mouths. BIG TIME!

The giant looks startled, but bows to the couple next in line, executes a snazzy military turn, and starts toward me.

I want to die.

My cover's blown before I can even get into the party.

I look at my feet still on the edge of the red carpet.

Should I step back onto the parking lot? How long will it take for the car to return and whisk me away?

I lift a foot and hold it over the pavement as I scan the parking lot. I spot the Gecko car barreling towards me. While I can't see his eyes through his dark sunglasses, I can feel his lizard's gaze lock onto my foot, the heel of my flip-flop perilously close to touching the road.

Go or stay?

One shot, one dance. That was my wish.

I risk looking back. The giant is almost to me when another man sidles next to him.

"It's okay, Moki," he says. "The lady is with me."

The mountain pauses mid-stride. "You sure, Jerry?"

"I got this. Thanks, guys," Jerry says and holds out his arm.

The valet nods and moves to the next car at the curb.

When I slip my hand into the crook of Jerry's elbow, he tucks it tight. From the corner of my eye, I see the Gecko car swerve away.

"Okeydokey," says the mountain. His eyes widen when they meet mine. "Wow, laulau, Jerry. She's cherry like a '57 Chevy. You're a lucky man."

He snaps off a salute. "Ma'am."

One complicated three-step about-face and he's striding back to the archway.

I feel the laughter Jerry's fighting to stifle as it rumbles in his chest. He turns and leads me away from the red carpet.

"Cherry like a '57 Chevy?" I say. "Really?"

He shoots me a look. "It's a compliment."

"Cherry like a classic car?"

"Moki works in a body shop straightening fenders all day. To him, something particularly fine is cherry." Jerry takes my hand off his elbow and twirls me around, giving a low whistle.

A potted hibiscus lining the walkway twitches.

I snatch my hand away. "Women are not dogs to be whistled at."

'Ilima pops into my head.

Maybe some of us are.

Can't think about that now.

Jerry cocks his head to the side, a slow smile pulling at his lips. "Moki's right. You look cherry—like you stepped out of an ad from the 1960s."

"You and that wolf-whistle belong in the '60s."

"This is Lauele. Sometimes there's not much difference."

"Cherry and Jerry, sitting in a tree, k-i-s-s—" sings a voice from the behind the potted plant.

"Knock it off, Luna!" I hiss.

"What?" Jerry asks.

"Nothing," I say.

I hear Luna giggle as his footsteps retreat.

Jerry leads me around the back of the tent to the area near the makeshift kitchen. There's an open doorway, and we pass through it and into the main tent. As I look around, I realize we're standing behind the stage.

Wires and cables run everywhere. Off to the side is an audio mixing board and monitors, the dials bouncing to the rhythm of the band playing on stage. Standing behind the loudspeakers that are pointed toward the crowd, it's surprisingly quiet backstage.

Jerry says, "Don't worry. This is one of the servers' entrances. You really didn't want to be announced, did you?"

I shake my head. "My stepmonster didn't want me here tonight."

"No! Not want you? Impossible." He clutches my hand to his chest like a B movie hero.

My heart leaps.

Chill out, Rell. He's joking.

'Ilima's right. I can't make this too easy.

I pull away.

"You mean the impossible boxes at the airport weren't a big enough clue that I'm not the favorite daughter?"

"They did make me wonder."

A waiter with a loaded tray rushes through the door. "Excuse me," he says. "Pupus coming through!"

"Oh, sorry," I say and step aside.

The waiter rolls his eyes at me. "The party's on the other side of the stage, people. This area is for staff only. If you love birds want a little privacy, head to the beach."

"Lighten up, Renten," Jerry says. "No act."

Renten sniffs. "Some of us are working, Jerry. Don't you have cars to park?"

Jerry stamps his foot and fakes a charge. Renten squeals and quickly rounds the stage.

"Yeah, that's what I thought," Jerry calls.

Cedar, cinnamon, cloves, and wintergreen mints.

I lace my fingers so I can't reach out and run my fingers through his hair.

Do I really need the car to bring me back to Poliahu's? Maybe walking home wouldn't be so bad.

Maybe I don't have to go back there at all.

I glance at my dress.

I'm on borrowed time.

But how short could that towel be?

Naked and in public, Rell. Keep that in mind. Do not kiss him!

When Jerry turns to me, his wide grin fades when he sees the look on my face.

Awesome!

I probably have crazy stalker woman tattooed on my forehead.

"Rell—"

"I'm sorry, Jerry." The words rush out like a train wreck.

He purses his lips. "You say that a lot."

He's got great lips. Soft and pillowy and firm like—

"Rell?"

"What? Oh. Sorry."

"Stop saying that. I'm the one who's sorry about how I behaved at Piko Point."

I look down, confused.

Piko Point?

He tips my chin up. "You don't have anything to apologize for."

He's talking about the rock.

This conversation is going to suck.

I take a breath.

"No, I do. I was supposed to be watching Ana and Zel. I'm responsible for the disrespectful and disgraceful way they pushed—"

He places a finger against my lips. Warmth spreads like butterscotch from the pit of my stomach to the ends of my toes.

"Shhhhh. I was there, too," he whispers. "It's not your fault."

"But the rock?"

"I got it back where it belongs. I actually think Pohaku enjoyed the swim."

He brushes a strand of hair from my cheek. My knees go weak. Those lips look so soft.

"...'Ilima?" he asks.

Crap. I missed something.

"'Ilima the dog?" I say.

It's his turn to look confused. "Yeah, the yellow dog at Piko Point. I haven't seen her. That sister of yours—"

"—stepsister—" I say.

"—Ana—" he says.

"—Zel—" I say.

"—whatever. One of those demons kicked 'Ilima really hard. I went to check on her later, but I couldn't find her. Uncle Kahana says she's missing. Have you seen her?"

"Uh, no," I say, eyes wide and face blank.

I should get an Oscar.

On stage, the song ends. The room applauds. Someone calls, "Hana hou! Hana hou!"

I raise an eyebrow at Jerry.

"It means they want more."

The singer says, "Ah, mahalo plenny, everyone. On behalf of Uncle Tiko, Uncle Butchie, and the rest of the band, I want to thank Get Wet Prosthetics for having us here tonight."

"Hana hou, Tuna! Hana hou!"

The singer turns to the band. "You guys wanna do one more?"

"Shoots," says the bass player. "Let's do *Ahe Lau Makani.*"

Back into the microphone, Tuna says, "One last song. Everybody out on the dance floor. Shake some loose change out of your pockets for the surf camp. Uncle Butchie, take us home."

The lead guitarist counts off. "One-two-three, one-two-three." The band swings into the intro.

"Is that a waltz?"

"Yeah," says Jerry.

"That's going to get everyone dancing? Not *YMCA* or *Boot Skootin' Boogie* or—"

"This is Lauele, remember?"

Through a seam in the backdrop, I see people grab partners and head to the area in front of the stage. Young, old, and everyone in between shuffle in modified boxed-steps.

In the soft glow of lantern light, it's magical.

Jerry takes my hand, the challenge clear in his eyes.

"No way. You waltz?" I say.

He puts his left hand on my waist. "Don't worry. I'll be gentle."

"Ha!" I put a hand on his shoulder. "Try to keep up."

We sway for a couple of beats, then his palm gently presses me backward, and we're off. He leads me in a few simple steps, and I follow with ease.

"You've done this before," he says.

"Six years of dance lessons."

"I thought you went to a fancy all-girls school."

"Yep. That means I can lead, too. Need a few pointers?"

He pulls me closer. "Oh, no, babe. We're just getting started."

He lengthens his stride, and we glide and swoop, my heart pounding one-two-three, one-two-three. He spins me in double-time, and I keep my eyes glued to his face, the one thing in sharp focus as the rest of the world whirls by. He pulls me tighter to his chest. I inhale cedar, cinnamon, cloves, and wintergreen mints.

One-two-three, one-two-three.

Ocean waves. Sand between my toes. Sunlight and tradewinds caressing my hair.

One-two-three, one-two-three.

Stepping over tide pools at Piko Point. Yellow tangs and snowflake eels. Feathery corals and translucent fins.

One-two-three, one-two-three.

As the song reaches the chorus, he signals for a dip.

One-two—

CRASH.

We tumble to the floor, the strands of my lei tangling between us.

"Rell! Are you okay?"

I feel a tug on my foot. I try to lift my leg, but my flip-flop is caught on a cable. As I kick it off, I realize my dress is riding high on my thighs. I quickly sit up and tug the hem down.

"Oh, yeah," I mutter. "This is much more practical than high-heels and poufy skirts. Bloody 'Ilima!"

"'Ilima? She's here?"

"No, she didn't get in the Gecko car with me."

"Rell, look at me. I need to check your eyes. Did you hit your head?"

"No. Just injured my pride." I gather my flip-flop and slip it back on. "Are you okay?" I ask.

He rolls to his side and props his head in his hand. "It feels like the scrape on my knee might be bleeding again."

"Oh, Jerry! I'm—"

He shakes his head. "Nope. You're not allowed to

say that anymore. The tragedies of the world aren't your fault."

"Tragedies of the world?" I grin.

He sits up and bumps my shoulder with his. "I meant comedies of the world. If it makes you feel better, you can take the blame for the trip. See you next fall."

"But you were leading!"

"I accept your apology," he says.

I punch his shoulder.

"Abuse! Abuse!"

"Right."

He laughs and wiggles his fingers menacingly. "Tickle retaliation!"

"Don't you dare—"

"Here's your mic, Ms. Watanabe."

Three people enter backstage and stand by the audio board.

"Call me Regina," says my stepmonster. "Like Cher or Beyoncé."

"Oh, like in that movie—"

"I have no idea what you're talking about," she says in a voice icicle cool. "There's only one Regina."

Regina?

"Eep!" I squeak and dive under the stage. Jerry hesitates for a split second, then slides next to me.

"They can't see us here," he whispers.

I'm too afraid to do more than nod.

Regina and Mr. Lucius stand near the stage stairs. An audio tech fiddles with Regina's mic. At the audio board he says, "Can you give me a little test?"

Regina says, "Test one, two, three."

Mr. Lucius says, "Eeney, meenie, miny, mo."

The audio tech watches the dials and frowns. "Mr. Lucius, could you repeat that please?"

"Catch a tiger by the toe."

The audio tech pats his pockets and looks around. "Your battery is low. I'm going to have to get a new one from the truck. Be right back."

As he disappears outside, Regina puts her hand on her hip. "The incompetence of these islanders is stunning."

I feel Jerry bristle.

Sorry, Jerry. My stepmonster's a jerk.

"A few more hours," Mr. Lucius says, "and it will all be over. Once the deal's done, you don't have to stay on this rock."

Regina lowers her voice. "The bribe worked?"

"There are no bribes, Regina. Only meaningful campaign contributions."

Jerry and I exchange a glance. He pulls his phone out of his pocket and hits record.

"And was our contribution meaningful?"

"Very. Once the permits for the surf camp's access road and utilities are filed with the county, the planning commission will be forced to approve our development behind it. It's just a matter of paying the filing fees. We're prepared to cover whatever doesn't get raised tonight."

From her purse, Regina pulls out some lipstick and starts smearing it along her lips. "Don't be too hasty, Lucius. Let them sweat and be grateful when we save their project. Public gratitude now will make it impossible for anyone to believe they didn't know about the eighty story high-rise we're building on the property behind them."

Jerry sucks in his breath so fast, I'm afraid they'll hear us. He holds the phone closer to them.

Mr. Lucius says, "Marketing is ready to go. Did you see the mock-ups of the sales campaign? We're positioning it locally as bringing jobs and technology to a blighted economy."

"Technology? That sounds expensive," says Regina.

"We're donating a few computers and upgrading the internet connection to the high school. That's it."

"Because we care," Regina says.

"Of course."

I want to smack the smirk right off his face.

"In the Euro and Asian markets we're positioning the development as the perfect island escape—a real life Bali Hai. We've already shot the beauty scenes of the beaches for the media campaigns." He sighs. "But have you thought this through, Regina? Do you really want an ugly, low budget surf camp of cripples to be the first thing your clients see?"

Regina laughs, and it's the sound of nails on a chalkboard and the last wormy apple as it falls off a tree.

"You're funny, Lucius. The camp is never going to be built. With my development, taxes and land values are going sky high. My analyst predicts that most of the land will be in foreclosure in less than five years. I'm going to own all of Lauele."

"I still don't understand, Regina. Other than the beach, there's nothing here. The only store or restaurant for miles is Hari's."

She puts away her lipstick and rubs her lips

together. Her mouth is shiny and red, like she's chewing glass.

"The first thing I'm going to do is knock down that ugly convenience store across the street and build a nice, modern natural foods kind of place."

"The lot's too small. You won't have parking."

"We'll raze the beach pavilion and expand the parking lot on this side. Once everything's private, there won't be a need for public works anymore."

Mr. Lucius holds up his hand. "The beach laws are ridiculous in Hawaii, Regina. You have to allow public access—even through private land."

"People won't come if the entire area's gated. We'll keep the riffraff out. Even the beaches will belong to the Bali Hai tenants."

"I don't think we can make that—"

"You can and you will. Increase our campaign contributions if necessary," she snaps.

Waving a black box and cord, the audio tech slips through the doorway. "Got a whole new set-up right here, Mr. Lucius."

"About time," mutters Regina.

The audio tech replaces Mr. Lucius's mic and pack.

"Let's test again," he says.

"If he hollers, let him go," Mr. Lucius says.

"Perfect." He places the old set next to the audio board. "Regina? Can you give me one last check?"

"Eeney, meenie, miny, mo."

Above us, the waltz fades. As the applause dies, the band scurries down the stairs and exits backstage. A woman's voice says, "Mahalo, gang. Before we get started with the auction, Uncle Kahana wants me to introduce someone who has become dear to our hearts: Regina Watanabe. Aunty Regina!"

"Aunty Regina?" Regina hisses. "Cow, I'm not related to you. These people!"

"Mic-ay on-ay," whispers Mr. Lucius. "Smile!"

Regina's fake smile doesn't reach her eyes.

Maybe it's not Botox.

As the woman exits stage right, Regina and Mr. Lucius climb the stairs and enter stage left. The audience is still applauding when the woman stops backstage and bends down.

"Howzit, Jerry," she says.

"Hey, Tuna," he says. "This is Rell."

"Aloha, Rell. I like your lei. Don't stay under the

stage too long. Get plenny spiders. Laters, gangies." She waves with just her thumb and pinky outstretched as she heads outside.

I turn to Jerry, eyes wide in the darkness. "How—"

He shrugs. "It's Tuna. We used to call her Tunazilla when we were kids. Voice of an angel, body of a linebacker. She just knows things."

Above us, Regina begins speaking.

"As you know, Watanabe Global has deep roots in this community. From the first moment I heard about the International Abilities Surf Tournament and its goal of expanding into a surf camp, I knew this project was exactly aligned with everything Watanabe Global stands for. Its value is immeasurable—"

"My father would never have torn down a community for money," I say. "She's going to ruin Lauele."

"There won't be a Lauele," Jerry says.

"This is my community, too. I've got to stop her."

"Rell—"

I grab Jerry's cell phone, crawl out from under the stage, pick up the abandoned mic set, and switch it on. There's enough juice in the batteries to make the needles bounce.

Suck it, Regina!

I hold the mic next to Jerry's phone and press play.

Nothing.

I press again.

Nothing.

I look closer.

Locked!

"Jerry, what's your password?"

"Ua mau ke ea o ka 'aina i ka pono."

"What?"

"Just hand me my phone."

Jerry stands next to me, flicking his fingers over his phone screen.

"Ready," he says.

"Let's do this!"

The file starts to play, but nobody can hear it over the loudspeakers.

"The battery's too weak," Jerry says. "Cut the other mics and boost it through the board."

I pull down the audio faders for Regina and Mr. Lucius's mics, cutting her off mid-sentence.

This is for you, Mama.

For you and our 'ohana.

I twist a dial and bring up the volume on the mic I'm holding above the cell phone.

"Is this better?" my voice booms over the loud-speakers.

"Rell?" shouts Regina from the stage.

Over the speakers, Regina's recorded voice says, "The camp is never going to be built. With my develop-ment, taxes and land values are going sky high. My analysist predicts that most of the land will be in fore-closure in less than five years. I'm going to own all of Lauele."

Chaos explodes.

The audio tech comes flying backstage. "What are you guys doing?" he shouts. "Get away from that equipment!"

Jerry steps in front me. "Just listen, Darin! The whole thing is a scam."

"Jerry—"

"LISTEN!"

Darin pauses.

Regina's voice says, "We'll keep the riffraff out. Even the beaches will belong to the Bali Hai tenants,"

Darin mouth drops. "Oh my—"

Regina and Mr. Lucius come flying backstage.

"Stop this immediately!" shrieks Regina. Her lipstick's smeared in a long red streak across her chin. Her hands go to her hair. "I demand that you give that illegal recording—"

"Fake illegal recording," shouts Mr. Lucius. "This is a fraudulent attempt to malign my client!

Darin stands next to Jerry, blocking access to the cell phone.

"Play that again, Jerry," he says. "I wanna know which politician we're impeaching."

Regina spots me cowering behind the guys.

"This is all your fault, Rell! When I get through with you—"

I turn and flee.

2 0

My foot barely touches the asphalt in the parking lot before the Gecko car screeches up. The valet runs up, but I'm faster. I fling open the door and jump into the backseat.

"Rell!" shouts the valet, "Is it true? Is Watanabe Global planning to build a huge—"

"Yes!" I say. "Sorry!"

I slam the door shut.

"Hit it!"

The driver snaps my head back as he accelerates out of the parking lot, smoke billowing behind.

The whole way to the house, I shake.

I stare out the windows at the empty beaches and modest homes that line the main road. The moon shines over the ocean, the light reflecting off coconut trees and hibiscus hedges as we speed by. I burn each image into my brain, trying to create a lifetime of memories in just a few minutes.

I can never come back.

None of this is real. It's all a giant chess match to get a high-rise development approved in Lauele. My father's company is planning to turn sleepy Lauele into an exclusive version of Waikiki. Regina never planned to support the surf camp. She just wanted the infrastructure permits approved so she could build her high-rise condominiums.

They must hate us.

I hate us.

Even if Jerry convinces people that I had nothing to do with it, there's no way I can show my face around here again.

Goodbye, Jerry.

It's probably best we never kissed.

The driver doesn't bother pulling into the driveway. He just whips up next to the gate and slams on the brakes. The locks on the backdoors pop open when I touch the door handle.

"Thanks," I say as I swing my legs and step outside. "I appreciate—"

SLAM!

The door rips out of my hand as the car takes off like a cockroach when the kitchen light comes on.

"Hey!" I'm so angry, I step out of my flip-flops and fling them after the car.

They miss by a mile.

Story of my life.

"Happy eighteenth birthday to me. It's all downhill from here."

All the lights are on in the house. It should be cheery and bright, but it feels cold and sterile. I shut the front door and blow on the decorative glass pane set in the middle. Mist coalesces, the patterns as delicate as a snowflake.

That's frost, I swear.

Inside the house is the faint scent of smoke. As I walk through the entry, I hear wood crackle and snap. I follow the sounds to the dining room and discover a roaring fire in the fireplace. Two white wingback chairs flank the fire on either side. Between them is a small table overflowing with a coffee service and trays. 'Ilima the woman is sitting in the chair to the right, a teacup and saucer balanced in her lap.

"Back so soon?" she says. "He must not have been a very good dancer."

"Can you get me to the airport?"

She takes a sip from her cup and watches me over the rim. "Where are your shoes?"

"Really? That's what you're concerned about?"

She shifts and curls her feet beneath her. "Come sit by the fire. Poliahu loves the cold, but she's mindful of the comfort of her guests." She gestures to the coffee service. "There are cookies, cake, sandwiches. Have a bite of something. Your blood sugar's low."

"How would you know?"

"Your smell."

"That's ridiculous."

She shrugs. "It's true. You haven't eaten a meal in hours. Your body tells me it's hungry by the sickly-sweet smell that's coming off you in waves."

"It's probably the flowers you're smelling."

"Nope. It's you. I've learned a lot about humans living with Kahana."

"You and Uncle Kahana?"

"Get your mind out of the gutter. It's not like that." She takes another sip, her eyes never leaving me. "Sit," she says. "You're making me nervous."

When I sit down, she hands me a plate of cookies and a teacup. "Liliko'i biscuits. I think you call them passion fruit cookies. Hold out your cup, and I'll pour."

"That's okay. I don't like tea or coffee," I say.

"Good, because this is hot chocolate." When she tips the pot, the chocolate pours out as rich and thick as molten lava. She fills my cup only halfway. "So you can dunk," she says.

"What—"

"Uh-uh. No talk. Eat."

I'm too tired and hungry to argue.

The cookie is crisp like shortbread with a thin layer

of passion fruit jam on the top. I dunk one into the hot chocolate, and it clings to the cookie like a hug.

I gently blow, then bite.

Ohhhhh," I moan. "I forgive you everything."

She grins like the Cheshire cat drinking cream. "Eat, child. We'll talk later."

I'm not sure how long I sit there, but when I'm done, the platters are empty. Little pies filled with coconut pudding, rolled pastries filled with cream and candied pineapple, tiny sandwiches filled with watercress and cucumber—I eat them all.

"More?" 'Ilima says.

"I couldn't."

She wrinkles her nose. "Well, at least you don't stink of hunger anymore." Setting her cup down, she sits forward and leans close.

"Bali Hai," she says. "The name isn't even Hawaiian."

"I didn't know about the development."

"But now you do." 'Ilima leans back in her chair. "Regina's bringing modern jobs and prosperity to backward Lauele."

"No, she's not."

"Are you sure? You're Rell Watanabe of Watanabe Global."

"My mother was a Mahope. This is my 'ohana."

'Ilima's eyes narrow. "'Ohana is an easy word to say when you'll get on a plane tomorrow."

I rock back in my chair. 'Ilima's words sting as harshly as if she'd slapped me.

Oh, come on! What am I supposed to do?

"I'm only eighteen!" I say.

She picks up her cup and takes a sip. "Yes, you're not a child any longer," she says.

"You mean I'm responsible?"

"When you claim the privileges of 'ohana, you also accept the responsibilities."

Jerry's words pop into my head.

"No one goes hungry," I say. "That's what you're getting at?"

'Ilima smiles.

"Jobs feed people. You think the jobs are important. You think what I did tonight to stop the development was wrong."

'Ilima takes another sip, her eyes never leaving my face.

I take a deep breath.

"I know you're powerful. You can probably turn me into a frog or something. But I don't agree. Jobs are not more important than people. There is more to life than money. Regina may still find a way to build her high-rise, but I'm going to do everything I can to make sure it's not on my mother's land in Lauele."

'Ilima's eyes crinkle. "A frog? Is that how you see yourself?"

"I…no," I say.

"Say ribbit."

"No!"

'Ilima's mouth quirks. "C'mon. I want to hear you say ribbit."

"I'm not going to say it."

"Why?"

"Because I'm not a frog!"

"Because you're not a frog. I wonder, Rell, if I held

up a mirror in the moonlight now, would you recognize the real you?"

Seriously?

We're back to mirrors and moonlight?

Shoot me now.

'Ilima takes one look at my face and bursts into laughter.

"Ah, child. Clearly, you're not made for poufy dresses, even if you don't realize that yet."

"Is Bali Hai the reason you did all of this?"

"Oh, no. That's merely a bonus."

Bonus?

The fire crackles. 'Ilima reaches out with the poker and pushes a log deeper into the flames.

"That's better. Nice and hot," she says. "You danced with the boy."

"Yes."

"But you didn't kiss him."

"No."

Her eyes gleam. "Then where are your shoes?"

I take a deep breath. "Out in the middle of the street."

"Why?"

"I threw them at the car."

"Why?"

"Because the driver almost ran me over when I was getting out."

'Ilima sits back and bites her lip. "You left my birthday gift in the street?"

I rise. "I'm sorry. That was thoughtless. You've been very kind to me. I'll go get them now."

She crosses her legs and rests her head against the

chair. "There's no need," she says, "since you've shown me you've no use for my gifts."

I flinch as wet hair tumbles down my back. In my hands is a washcloth. One side of my body is warm from the fireplace, the other is freezing.

Freezing because I'm naked.

I flip the washcloth, pulling it this way and that, trying to cover all of my bits and pieces, but it's no use.

'Ilima rolls her eyes. "Modern humans are so uptight. You would've thanked me if you'd kissed him."

I step behind my chair. "Where are my clothes?"

"Where did you leave them?"

"In the dryer."

"Then that's where you should check."

I spin around and head to the laundry room.

Bloody, bloody dog!

As I put on my clothes, I hear her chuckling. Yanking my shirt over my head, I storm back into the dining room.

"You think this is funny?"

"Are you mad because I didn't fold and iron your clothes?" She sniffs. "I'm not your maid."

"Or my fairy godmother. You said that. Who are you? Why are you doing this to me?"

'Ilima stands. In the flickering of the firelight, she grows, filling the space around her until her head brushes the ceiling. "I do things to achieve my own purposes," she says. "I pay my debts and collect those owed to me. This night isn't over."

The front door swings open with a force that shatters the glass pane in the center.

"RELL! You will come here this instant!"

The last word is a hiss no human can make.

I have just enough time to see 'Ilima shrink back into a dog and curl up beneath a chair before my stepmonster stalks into the room.

"Traitor!" she shrieks. "After all I've done for you. I paid for your schooling, your room and board, and the clothes on your back!"

She grabs a vase from the sideboard and throws it at me. I duck, and it shatters against mantel. "No more! Do you hear me? No more!"

I square my shoulders and pull my head high. With nothing left to lose, she has no power over me.

"Go back to the hell you crawled from, Regina! I don't need you or your money."

"Oh, no? Your fancy school has been cancelled. You have nowhere to go."

"I can stay with the headmaster and his family. I've done it before during the holidays. They won't mind. I can stay with them until I get a job and can pay my own way."

Regina cackles. "You think you stayed with the headmaster's family because they liked you? No, Rell. I paid them to take you in. They don't care about you. You're just a paycheck to them."

"I don't believe you. When I fly home—"

"You won't."

"What?"

Regina grins and my blood chills. She wags her manicured finger at me and speaks so softly I can barely hear her. "You're not going back to school, Rell. You're not well. After the way you treated your sisters today and the lies you told at the auction, well, it's obvious you're a very troubled girl. I have a very special place in mind, a place that will heal your damaged mind. It's a lockdown facility in Taiwan. We'll reassess after the second or third round of electric shock therapy, but the doctors are very keen on some new brain surgery techniques they'd like to try."

My mouth goes dry.

"You wouldn't."

She crosses her arms. "I already have."

"You can't."

"I can. I did."

Her phone beeps, and she glances at the text message.

"The medical crew is on its way. I just received confirmation of straight jacket restraints and meds to make you compliant. See for yourself."

She holds out the phone, but when I move to take it, she yanks it away.

"You really think I'd give you my phone? That's your problem, Rell. You think everyone is as stupid as you."

"No. She thinks everyone is as kind as she is," says Uncle Kahana from the doorway. He steps to the side. "Watch out, Avery. There's glass on the floor here."

Mr. Me'e walks into the room, a folded paper in his hands. "Hello, Rell. Remember me?" he says.

I nod.

"What are you doing here? You work for me!" Regina says.

"I quit."

"You can't quit. I have your firm on retainer. Nobody treats me like this." She punches buttons on her cell phone. "I'm calling Lucius right now."

"Knock yourself out," Mr. Me'e says.

"And I'm calling the police! You are all trespassing!" Regina flounces to the other side of the room. "Lucius? I need you immediately!"

Uncle Kahana says, "Is she always like this?"

Mr. Me'e nods.

"I think the surf camp dodged a bullet."

'Ilima thumps her tail.

"'Ilima! I've been looking for you everywhere!" Uncle Kahana says.

'Ilima chuffs.

"Fine," says Uncle Kahana. "We'll talk about it later."

Mr. Me'e hands me the paper. I unfold it. It's the paper I signed in this very room so many lifetimes ago.

"Rell, I didn't make copies of this document like Regina and Mr. Lucius wanted. That's the original. You have no idea what you signed, do you?"

"Something that allows Regina to pay for my schooling. If I don't sign these papers every year, she can't pay my tuition. I don't earn enough cleaning the school kitchen to pay for more than half my board."

Mr. Me'e sighs. "That's what I was afraid of. Rell, those papers you signed every year were your consent —your permission—for Regina to continue to act as your legal guardian."

"Isn't that what I said?"

"No." He turned to Uncle Kahana. "It's as I suspected. She really doesn't understand."

Uncle Kahana comes to me and kneels at my feet. He takes my hands in his and looks me in the eye.

"Rell, when you signed those papers every year, you told the courts that you wanted Regina to be in charge of you and your estate. Your father set his will up so you could choose. Regina was not your guardian until you chose her."

In an instant, I'm twelve years old. Daddy is dead. The house is full of somber people wearing black. Regina and Mr. Lucius take me into Daddy's office. Regina hands me a brochure with pictures of horses and smiling girls.

"Wouldn't you rather be there? Look at this school."

I can't think. The black lace on my dress is itchy, and my shoes pinch.

Mr. Lucius says, "All you need to do is sign right here, Rell. You can be there tomorrow."

I pick up the pen and scrawl my name.

I blink back the tears. "All these years I could've had another guardian? But no one wanted me!"

Mr. Me'e says, "That's not true, Rell. Lots of your father's friends and family wanted you. Your mother's family, too. Before anyone had a chance to talk with you, you disappeared. When people pushed, Mr. Lucius just showed them the paper you signed naming Regina as your guardian. Regina forbade anyone from contacting you at school."

"Rell, lots of people have been waiting for this day," Uncle Kahana says. "Do you know why?" I shake my head. "Today you turned eighteen. You no longer need a guardian. Anyone who wants to contact you can."

I can't breathe.

Mr. Me'e nods. "I have a stack of birthday cards in my car dating back to when you turned thirteen." He looks down. "But I didn't give them to you because you signed that paper today giving Regina power of attorney over you and your estate."

"This paper makes her the boss of me?"

"Yes. And your estate."

My head is spinning. It's too hot near the fire.

"You said my estate. What's my estate? Money? Did Daddy leave me enough to finish school? Is there enough for me to go to college?"

Mr. Me'e and Uncle Kahana exchange a look.

"Rell," says Uncle Kahana, "your estate is Watanabe Global."

Mr. Me'e nods. "You control the whole thing."

Sirens wail in the distance, getting closer as they climb the mountain. It's either the police coming to arrest Uncle Kahana and Mr. Me'e or the Taiwanese doctors with straitjackets and needles coming to take me away.

Before I can say anything, Regina rushes back across the room, waving her cell phone at me.

"I hope you're satisfied. Lucius is filing so many charges against all of you, you won't see daylight for a century."

"You planned to steal my mother's land and build high-rise condos on it. You were going to raise the taxes so high, people would beg you to buy them out for pennies on the dollar," I say.

"Rell—" Regina says.

"You were never going to build the surf camp," I say. "You just wanted the permits. But the joke's on you, Regina. Because of what you said tonight, the auction was never held. Without the auction, there aren't any funds to pay the fees."

"You see what I mean, gentlemen? Rell is delusional. She thinks there's a big conspiracy. The truth is, as a show of good faith, Watanabe Global just paid the fees for the surf camp's permits. Everything is in order."

"Not quite." I stand and hold out the paper. "Do you see this, Regina? It's the paper I signed this afternoon. It's the only copy."

Regina lunges at me.

I yank the paper away.

"Did you really think I'd let you touch it? That's your problem, Regina. You think everyone is as evil as you."

I wad up the paper and toss it into the fire.

"NOOOO!" Regina screams, pushing me aside and plunging her hands into the flames.

"Grrrr," growls 'Ilima as she shoots out from under the chair and chomps down on Regina's arm.

Regina screams and pulls her charred hands out of the flames.

Uncle Kahana grabs a bowl filled with floating gardenias and dumps the water over Regina's hands.

Regina falls to her knees, sobbing.

'Ilima retreats under the table, spitting and rubbing her tongue along the carpet.

All of this goes on, but I never take my eyes off the charring ball of paper until there is nothing left but ashes.

2 4

I'm sitting on Poliahu's front steps when Jerry walks up and sets my bag down beside me.

"Thanks," I say.

"I was going to give you your bag earlier, but you left in such a hurry."

He tosses a pair of flip-flops at my bare feet.

"I found these out in the road. I think they belong to you."

As I bend to put them on, he kneels at my feet.

"Allow me." He cups my heel in his hand and slips the strap between my toes. "Perfect fit. They must be yours."

"Because they wouldn't fit anyone else?"

He laughs. "Don't be silly. Slippahs fit everybody. That's why they're the official non-shoe of Hawaii." He nudges my leg. "Scoot over."

I slide over so he can sit next to me, and we watch as the EMTs load Regina into the ambulance.

Bright side: they got to use some of the sedatives she ordered for me.

Waste not, want not.

"Where are the twins?" Jerry asks.

"Aulani. They're enjoying a Disney Princess Sleepover Party. I'll pick them up tomorrow."

"What're you going to tell them?"

I sigh. "I don't know. That's tomorrow's problem."

"You're staying here alone?"

I shake my head. "No. Once Regina's on her way to the hospital, Mr. Me'e is taking me to a hotel in Waikiki."

"Or you can stay with me."

I look at him.

"I mean, with my family. My mom said to ask you. She's worried."

"'Ohana," I say.

"Of course."

"Calabash."

Jerry puts his arm around my shoulders. "Calabash," he says.

Uncle Kahana comes over and pecks me on the cheek. "Happy birthday, Rell."

"Thanks."

"I'll see you tomorrow. Come on, 'Ilima. Let's go home."

'Ilima rises slowly from the lawn, limping a little.

"Hey, what happened to you?" Uncle Kahana says.

She chuffs and jumps into his car.

"Kicked in the ribs?" Uncle Kahana says. "Who?"

'Ilima sits up on the front seat and locks eyes with me through the windshield.

In my head I hear her voice: *I pay my debts and collect those owed to me.*

I shiver.

No matter what, I need to make sure I'm never on 'Ilima's bad side.

"Cold?" says Jerry, pulling me closer.

I bury my nose in his shirt.

Cedar, cinnamon, cloves, and wintergreen mints.

"Rell?"

I raise my chin and capture his lips. At first, they're soft with surprise, but firm enthusiastically as our kiss deepens.

Cedar, cinnamon, cloves, and wintergreen mints.

And something a whole lot more.

He breaks the kiss and takes a deep breath. I snuggle back down, and he rests his chin on my head.

"I know who I am," I say.

"Oh? Is this a game? Am I supposed to guess?"

"I'm Rell Watanabe."

"Nice to meet you, Rell. I'm Jerry."

"And I know what I want."

I feel him hold his breath.

"I'm afraid to ask," he says.

I sit up and look him in the eye.

"I want to build a surf camp."

Events and characters in this story also appear in
One Boy, No Water
Book 1 of the Niuhi Shark Saga trilogy
and other Lauele Universe Stories by Lehua Parker.

TALKING STORY NEWSLETTER

Want to receive free bonus content, sneak peeks, special event announcements, writing tips from the Lehua Writing Academy, and exclusive perks on upcoming titles from Makena Press? Sign up for Lehua Parker's Talking Story Newsletter. You can change your subscription preferences at anytime. New subscribers get an exclusive welcome bonus.

Subscribe to
Talking Story Newsletter

http://www.lehuaparker.com/newsletter

ABOUT LEHUA PARKER

LEHUA PARKER writes speculative fiction for kids and adults that often explores the intersections of Hawaii's past, present, and future. Her published works include the Niuhi Shark Saga trilogy, Lauele Chicken Skin Stories, and Lauele Fractured Folktales, as well as plays, poetry, short stories, and essays.

As an author, editor, and educator trained in literary criticism and advocate of indigenous cultural narratives, Lehua is a frequent presenter at conferences, symposiums, and schools. Her hands-on workshops and presentations for kids and adults are offered through the Lehua Writing Academy.

Originally from Hawai'i and a Kamehameha Schools graduate, Lehua now lives in exile in the Rocky Mountains. During the snowy winters, she dreams of the beach.

Connect with her at:

www.LehuaParker.com

Subscribe to Talking Story Newsletter at
www.LehuaParker.com/newsletter

www.ingramcontent.com/pod-product-compliance
Lightning Source LLC
Chambersburg PA
CBHW062023190726

48284CB00014B/2637